THE MYSTERY OF HIDDEN HARBOR

In the Same Series:

THE MYSTERY OF HIDDEN HARBOR

BY JOHN STEPHEN DOHERTY

Illustrated by Charles Beck

WILDSIDE PRESS

Contents

CHAPTER ONE

Something Strange
Is Going On

Pete Dana leaned on the railing at the edge of the boat yard and looked out toward the sound. It was a perfect day. A warm sun beat down from a clear blue sky and a light breeze sent ripples across the waters of Hidden Harbor.

Below Pete, the gas float rocked gently. For the fifth time that day Pete looked at the new sign that had been put up the day before, the same day he had been graduated from high school. It stood just above the steps that led from the yard down to the gas float and said:

HIDDEN HARBOR BOAT YARD
—Pete & Wesley Dana—
GAS * ICE * FUEL
BAIT * STORAGE * REPAIRS

The new sign was the same as the old one, except for one new word—Pete's name.

Pete and his father looked like father and son. Both were tall, neither had an ounce of spare flesh. Their blond hair was almost the same color, but where the father's was turning gray Pete's was almost white from the sun.

Far across the water the buzz of a fast motor boat floated back to Pete. He turned and his eyes searched the entire harbor, but he could not see it.

Turning back to the yard, he saw his father painting a boat. And at the far end of the yard, Nick Zenos was piling up timbers. Nick was the Greek-American who had come to Hidden Harbor after a hitch in the Navy, to work at the yard.

Seeing them together, Pete wondered if he should be going off on a one-week camping trip. The new sign over his head reminded him that he was now a real partner in the yard. It didn't seem fair for Pete to have a vacation. But Wesley Dana had insisted.

"You have earned a few days off, Pete," he had said. "You did pretty well in your final grades. You are almost eighteen years old and you have a long life of work ahead of you. So do some fishing while you can. The work will be here when you come back."

Pete picked up his sleeping roll and sea bag full of clothes and equipment, and walked down to the float to put them in his sailboat. Dropping them in, he heard the sound of the fast motor boat again. As he started back to the main dock for his box of food, the sound of the boat grew louder. When he reached the upper dock and turned, Pete saw a red speed boat coming in to the boat yard's gas dock.

When the red boat was less than fifty yards out, it was still coming at full speed. Pete jumped back.

"Hey! Slow down!" he shouted.

Even as he called out, the driver's arm came up in a wave. At the last second, the man behind the wheel cut the power and threw the motor into reverse. As he neared the dock, he gunned the motor, bringing the boat to a sudden stop. With a roar, the boat rocked and a wave rolled across the gas float, soaking Pete's sneakers and pants.

Before Pete could say anything, the driver jumped out and on to the dock. He walked right past Pete. He wore clothes, Pete noticed, the way he handled a boat—loud and splashy. He paused on the dock.

"Make you jump, eh, boy?" he said. "Well, that's what this sick town needs—a shot in the arm! I told your father that the other day and he agreed with me." He gave Pete a big smile. "Fill her up, boy, and hop!"

He turned and was gone up into the yard, walking toward Wesley Dana. Pete was so surprised he just stood there without saying a word. Who was this character with the loud mouth, and how did he have the nerve to call Hidden Harbor "sick"? Pete loved his home town and he didn't like strangers finding fault with it.

9

Then Pete thought that the man probably was Jeffrey Fannin, who had rented the old factory at the far end of the harbor. Pete's father had told him that Fannin was opening a boat business—selling a line of red speed boats called Sea Sharks. One thing was sure, Jeffrey Fannin was a nut when it came to handling boats.

Still, it was none of his business, Pete thought. He filled the gas tank on the boat and made out a sales slip.

A minute later Fannin—if it was he—came down to the float, looked at the sales slip Pete gave him and handed Pete a couple of dollar bills. "Keep the change, boy," he said.

Then he jumped into his boat, started the engine and swung away from the dock in a wide turn, without looking where he was going. Fifty yards off the end of the dock he started moving at top speed through the fleet of boats in the mooring area. He paid no attention to the big red and white sign that said:

MOORING AREA
TOP SPEED
5 MPH

Finally, the red boat disappeared in the direction of the old factory. Pete walked up into the yard.

"Who is that?" he asked his father.

"You don't sound as if you thought much of him."

"Not the way he handles a boat."

Wesley Dana stepped back. "Well, Pete, I guess if you are selling speed boats you just naturally want to show people how fast they can go."

"We don't want that kind of boat man around here, do we, Dad?"

"We may not want him," Wesley Dana said, "but we sure need him."

Pete was surprised. "Why, for crying out loud?"

Wesley Dana turned and looked at his son. "Pete, Hidden Harbor needs business. And the Dana Boat Yard needs business. We need new life around here. Jeffrey Fannin may be just the man to give it to us."

Pete knew that what his father said made sense but it did not make him like Fannin any better.

"Did you see the way he came in through our fleet?"

"No, I did not," Wesley Dana said, "but I could tell by the sound that it was pretty fast."

"I will never forget how you read me the riot act when I did that once."

"Oh, he will learn!"

"And did you see that smile of his?" Pete asked. "It was about as honest as a sand shark's."

Wesley Dana paused again. "Come on, now, Pete, don't judge the man so soon. Give him a chance to learn. We need Jeffrey Fannin. Times are changing, Pete. And now that you are a full partner, you have to think of the boat yard."

Pete suddenly found the thought of being on vacation

—far from Jeffrey Fannin—a very pleasant idea indeed.

"I guess it is time to shove off," he said.

As they headed across the yard, Wesley Dana said, "Are you going to stay the week?"

Pete nodded. "I will if the weather holds."

They had reached the dock. Pete began to raise his main sail. Wesley Dana cast off the lines. The breeze picked up and Pete steered away from the dock.

"Check in every other day, just so I know you are all right," his father called.

"I will," Pete promised. He waved and his father waved back. Pete had the wind in his favor and was soon making good time.

Sailing across the water, Pete enjoyed watching for all the familiar signs. Hidden Harbor was a small town, with less than 10,000 people. Pete knew at least half of them by sight if not by name.

Around the rim of the harbor he saw the pine trees on the rocky slopes that ran down to the water's edge. At the east end, to Pete's left, were shallow water and the marsh. Few boats went there, but a deep channel led up to the old factory dock. Northwest of the factory the land became a sand bar that swung out into the Atlantic Ocean, and curved around to the west. It ended at Lighthouse Point, which marked the main channel into Hidden Harbor from the sea. This long sand bar was named the Dunes. It had no buildings on it, but was a public recreation area for all the people who lived in the town.

At the south end of the harbor was Fish Town, where the men of the fishing fleet lived and kept their boats. And all along the west shore, the town of Hidden Harbor ran right down to the edge of the water front. The public dock was there, for the use of visiting boats.

Pete's favorite place was the Dunes. With one side of it facing the ocean and the other facing the harbor, it had given Pete every kind of lesson that a boy could learn living on the edge of the sea. It had taught him about wind, weather, tides and storms. He knew every mood of the sea from violence to calm, and he could handle a small boat in any kind of sea.

When Pete was half way across the harbor, he remembered that the Professor would be on the Dunes. The Professor was John Nevins, a 30-year-old college teacher, and an expert on sea birds. He came to Hidden Harbor every summer to camp out. Pete had taught the Professor how to sail and the Professor had promised that this summer he would teach Pete to use skin diving gear.

Knowing that the Professor liked to make his camp at the east end of the Dunes, Pete pointed his sailboat that way. He could tie up at the end of the old factory dock and walk along the shore to find the Professor.

Ten minutes later, Fannin's huge red house boat came into view. As he drew closer, Pete decided he did not like it. The house boat did not look like a real boat, and the red color was too loud for his taste. Sailing past it, he was surprised to see no one around. Dropping the sails quickly as he reached the end of the dock beyond the house boat, Pete climbed up and threw a knot around a piling with his docking line. When another look around showed him that no one was there, he turned and walked toward the place where the Professor always made his camp.

He found it five minutes later, a large tent pitched in a spot sheltered from the wind.

"Hello!" he yelled. "Professor Nevins!"

There was no answer. The Professor, he guessed, must be over on the ocean side of the Dunes. Pete started climbing. Ten minutes later, he saw the Professor far down the beach, leaning over a small camp stove not far from where the waves washed up on the sand.

"Hi, Professor," he called out. "How are you?"

Professor Nevins turned, saw Pete and smiled. "Hello, Pete," he said. "Good to see you. I've been wondering where you were." They shook hands.

"I was just graduated from high school yesterday." Pete answered.

"That's right! Good for you. I guess you won't have much time for skin diving this summer, though, if you are going to work."

"I have a whole week," Pete answered. "But right now I want to put up my tent before it gets dark. How about having supper with me? Bring your stuff over."

"Sure! Always glad to share a good meal," the Professor said. He ran his hand across the top of his head, a habit he had when he was pleased. "In about half an hour?"

Waving good-by, Pete walked off.

When he reached the top of the dune behind the Professor's tent, Pete looked down at the calm waters of the harbor . . . and got the shock of his life.

His boat was gone.

Slipping and sliding, he ran down the steep slope to the edge of the water. Then he saw it. The sailboat was out on the water, almost a mile away, drifting quickly with the tide.

Pete realized instantly that if he did not get the boat soon, the tide would carry it out to sea. But first he wanted to see something. He ran to the end of the dock and picked up his docking line: it was worn through. Pete could not believe it, but he had no time to think any more about it then.

Running back off the dock, he started down the beach. Fifty yards along, he had to splash through the shallow water that linked the ocean and the harbor.

Beyond North Inlet, Pete settled down to steady running. In the time since he had first seen it, the boat had drifted another half mile.

At last, when he was less than a half mile from Lighthouse Point, Pete caught up with his boat. He saw that he was lucky. It was only about a hundred yards off the beach. Quickly, he pulled off his shirt and blue jeans and plunged in.

The cool water gave him a lift and he began swimming strongly toward the boat. When he reached it, he clung to the side, resting. The tide continued to carry the boat toward the sea. With one try, Pete pulled himself into the boat and lay there breathing hard.

In a moment he recovered, raised the sails, swung the boat around and started back toward the spot where he had left his clothes. Pulling the boat up on the beach, he quickly slipped into his jeans and shirt. Setting sail again, he headed for the old factory.

Fannin and a huge man with red hair were standing

on the end of the dock when Pete got there. One look at Fannin was all Pete needed. Without thinking twice, Pete shouted, "What's the idea of cutting my boat loose?"

Fannin smiled. "Aren't you being a little fast in accusing me?" He lifted the end of Pete's docking line. "This doesn't look to me as if it had been cut."

"I never lost a boat that way in my life!" Pete answered hotly. "That is brand new rope. It could not have worn through."

"It could not have, but it did," Fannin said, and threw the end of the docking line into the boat.

The huge man spoke up. "Look, kid, stay off this dock and stay away from this factory. This is private property. If you had kept your boat where it belongs, nothing would have happened to it." He paused. "Next time, maybe you won't be so lucky. Maybe you will lose your boat altogether."

Fannin cut in. "He is just giving you some good advice. We are busy around here and we don't have time for kids."

"Since when do you own the harbor?" Pete asked. "As far as I know, these are federal waters, open to everybody."

Fannin turned and walked off. "Come on, Bucko," he said. "This boy just won't learn."

Bucko pointed a finger at Pete. "You heard what the man said," he growled. Then he followed Fannin.

Pete could feel the blood rush to his face. He picked

up the breeze and headed for the place on the Dunes where he was going to make camp.

When the Professor arrived, he had a roaring fire going but his tent was still lying on the sand. It was almost dark.

"What happened, Pete?" he asked. "I came over twenty minutes ago and you weren't here."

As Pete finished telling his story, he said, "It must have been done on purpose!"

The Professor shook his head slowly. "You can't prove it, Pete. And the rope *was* worn through."

Pete nodded, but did not say anything. He had spoken to Fannin too soon, without thinking. Now he was doing the same thing with the Professor. He got busy with the food. In a few minutes he handed his friend a paper plate loaded with hot dogs and beans.

They ate in silence and, when they had finished, the Professor said, "Why don't you sleep in my tent tonight? It will give me a chance to show you the skin diving gear."

As they walked across the sand to the Professor's camp, the sky grew dark and the stars came out. Wading through North Inlet, they heard the sound of hammering echoing across the water from the house boat.

"Now why would they be hammering in the middle of the night?" Pete asked.

"Beats me."

"Something funny *is* going on over there," Pete said.

"Forget it, Pete," the Professor said. "Come on in and look over the equipment."

They were talking quietly when the shattering noise of a speed boat engine cut through the night air. They listened in surprise as the boat roared away from the dock and headed out into the middle of the harbor.

"Now do you believe me?" Pete asked. "Why would anyone go buzzing around like that in the dark?"

The Professor puffed on his pipe for a few seconds. Then he said, "I don't know, Pete, but that doesn't mean there is anything wrong. When you get to know Fannin you may find yourself laughing at your suspicions. Come on, let's hit the sack."

As Pete stretched out in the Professor's spare sleeping bag, the whole day went through his mind. His father had told him many times, "Pete, look before you leap. You have to *think first*, son, then act." Pete knew his father was right.

But even as he fell off to sleep, he thought, "Something strange is going on in Hidden Harbor. I have to find out what it is."

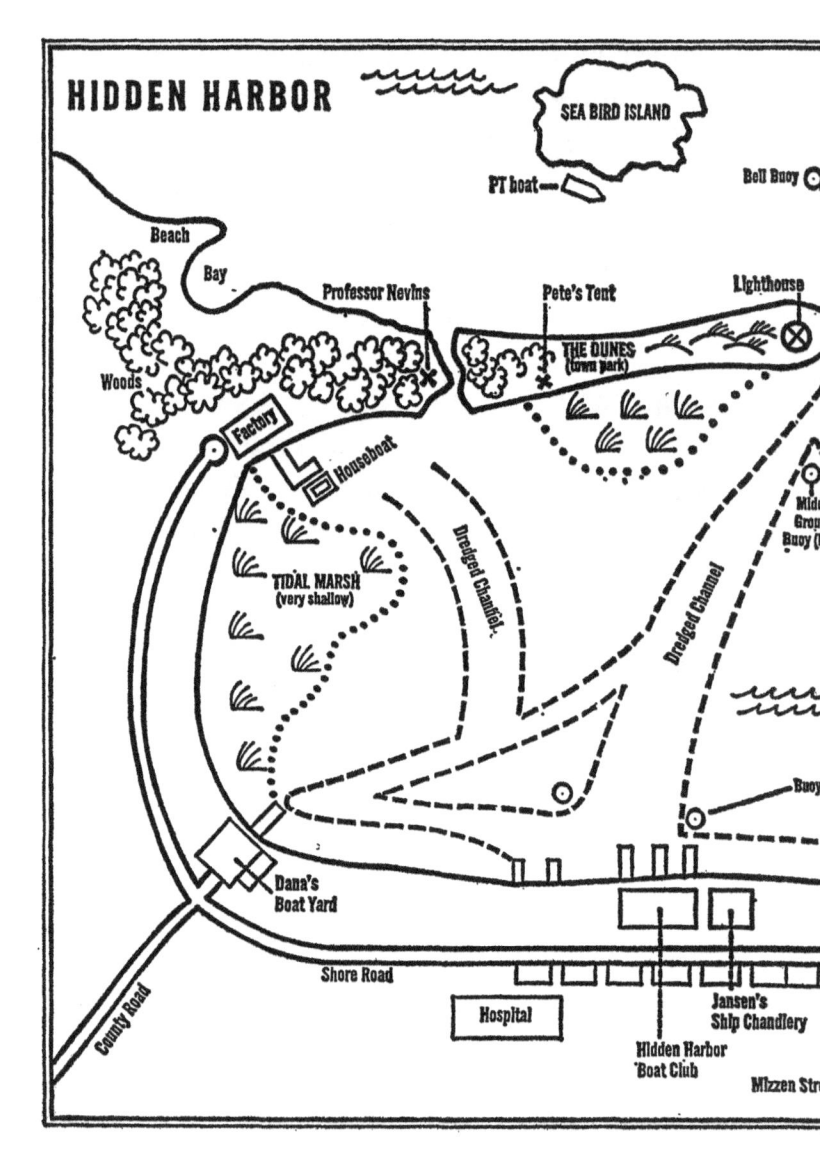

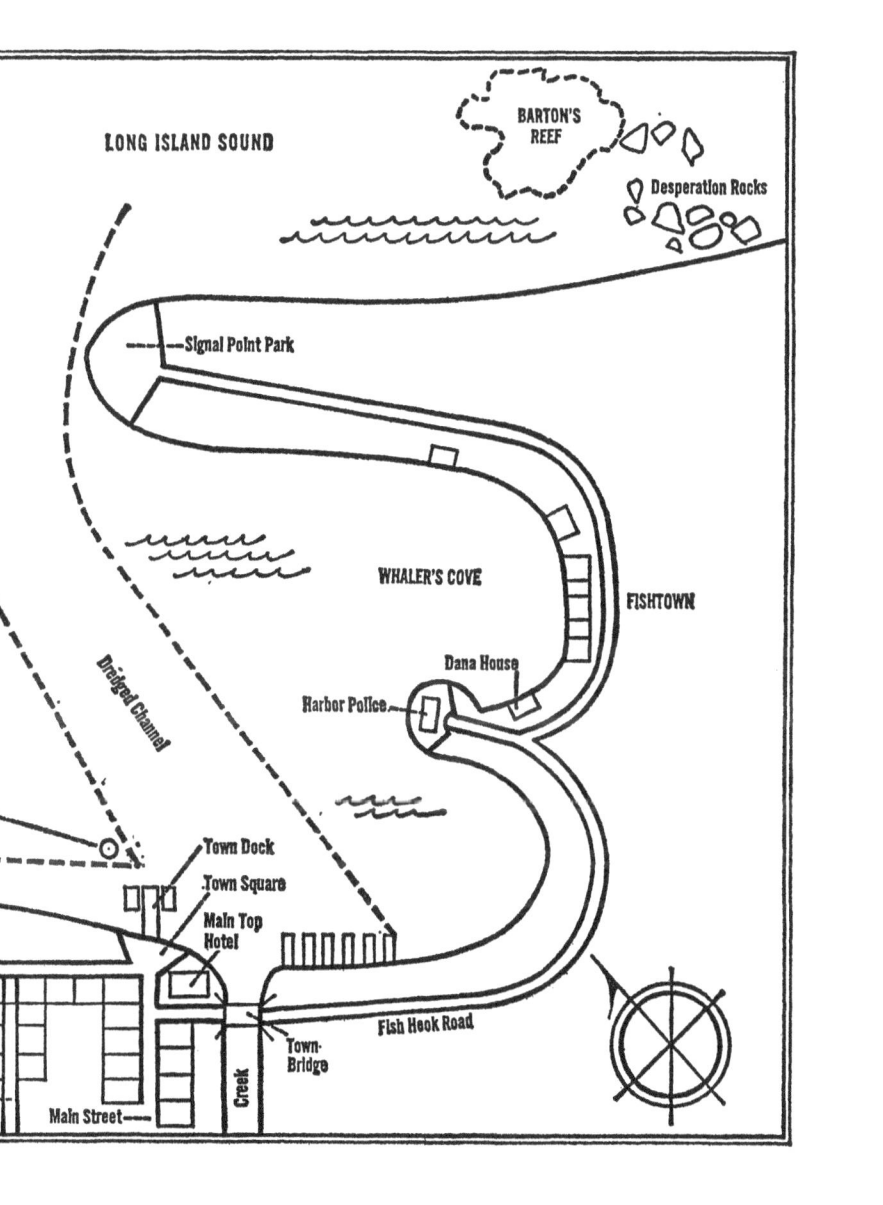

CHAPTER TWO

Keep Within the Law

Pete was up early in the morning. While the Professor cooked breakfast over an open fire, Pete took a quick swim. When he had dried himself and dressed, Professor Nevins handed him his breakfast of eggs and bacon, two slices of bread and a small mound of jelly.

"Nothing fancy," the Professor said, "but you won't starve."

They ate in silence for a few minutes.

"What are you going to do today?" Pete asked.

The Professor lit his pipe and leaned back against a log.

"My project this summer is to study the nesting habits of the sea birds living here in the marsh and out on Sea Bird Island. I finished two dozen nesting boxes and set them out during the Easter vacation. Today I'm going to

22

check them out in the marsh. In the next couple of weeks I hope the eggs will start hatching. Then I can study how the nests are built and how long the young birds use them."

"Want me to help you?" Pete asked.

"Thanks, Pete, but I had better do it alone. Even one person going into the marsh will frighten the birds. Two people will make it worse. Anyway, you have to put up your tent."

"All right," Pete said, "but I can help you with your boat."

Pete and the Professor went down to the edge of the water and Pete waded out to get the Professor's rowboat. It was tied between two posts just off shore so that it wouldn't be left high and dry when the tide went out.

Pete called back to the Professor, "Boy, you sure hit this boat a hard whack against something!"

"What are you talking about?"

"Your boat. You cracked a plank in it."

Pete pulled it in to shore. On one side there was a long scrape in the paint and under it a side plank was broken. Something had certainly hit the rowboat hard.

The Professor looked surprised. "I didn't do that," he said. "The boat was in perfect shape when I tied it up there yesterday afternoon."

Pete said, "I'll bet it happened while we were having supper."

"But how?"

"That speed boat," Pete said. "Remember? It made a run down this end."

"You mean Fannin?"

"Who else? It's just like him. Look!" Pete leaned over and pointed. "Looks like red paint to me, and red is the color of Fannin's boats."

"We don't even know for sure that it was Fannin's boat speeding around last night," the Professor told him.

"I do," Pete said. "I would bet my life on it."

"Is the boat going to leak?" the Professor asked.

Pete nodded. "Sure is."

"That's no good. I have to carry valuable instruments around in it."

Pete took a closer look at the damage. "We can fix it over at the yard in a couple of hours. I can have it back right after lunch."

The Professor smiled gratefully. "Fine. I can write up my reports while you are gone."

Pete pulled the boat through the shallow water down to his camp. Then he tied it behind his sailboat, raised sail and started across the harbor.

When he got to the boat yard, Nick was standing on the upper dock.

"Hi, Pete!" he yelled. "Did you catch only one?"

Pete grinned. "Sure, but look at the size of it."

When Pete told him what had happened, Nick raised his eyebrows. "Well, it *could* be Fannin with that red paint on it, but how can you be sure?"

24

Nick tied Pete's boat up to the main dock and raised the Professor's rowboat on to a sort of wooden cradle where he could get at it. Then he started the repair work.

"Where is Dad?" Pete asked.

"Went in to buy supplies," Nick told him.

By noon, when Wesley Dana returned to the yard, Pete was painting the new plank that had been put in.

"What happened?" his father asked Pete.

Pete explained. When he had finished, Mr. Dana paused for a moment.

"You can't be sure Fannin did it," he said. "And even if he did, how do you know he did it on purpose?"

Pete felt angry. He wanted to tell his father that Fannin was going to bring trouble to Hidden Harbor. But he knew that his father would say the same thing Nick and Professor Nevins had said.

When the paint on the repairs was dry enough, Pete once more towed the boat across the harbor.

"That was a quick job," the Professor called out as Pete came drifting in to the beach.

"Nick is pretty good," Pete agreed.

"And what is your special job?" Nevins asked.

"I am the gas float expert," Pete said, grinning.

The Professor laughed. "It's a little late for me to check all my nesting boxes this afternoon. How about your first skin diving lesson?"

"Great!" Pete agreed.

They brought the new gear down to the rowboat. Pete

carried the small motor from the tent and fastened it to the stern. He started the motor and turned to the Professor.

"Where to?" he asked.

"Go down past your camp toward Lighthouse Point. We need clear water and a sandy bottom."

Pete nodded and steered the boat to the west, toward Lighthouse Point.

"This looks pretty good," the Professor said. "How deep is it?"

Pete stopped the motor, picked up an oar from the bottom of the boat and pushed it down into the water.

"About up to my chest."

"Fine. Let's anchor," the Professor said.

Pete dropped the anchor and, when it caught, stripped down to a pair of swimming trunks. The Professor did the same and they dived into the water.

"All right, Pete," he said. "Let's start with the masks."

Professor Nevins showed Pete how to wet the inside of the glass face piece in the mask. "If you don't wet it," he said, "it may steam up when you stay under for a while." Then he showed Pete how to get a tight fit around the edges, so that no water would get in. After that, Pete swam under water. He was surprised at how clearly he could see.

Next, Pete tried on the rubber swim fins that fitted over his feet.

"They look funny," he told Professor Nevins, "but they sure help. With them, I could keep up with a fish."

"Don't bet on it," the Professor said, laughing. "But they do add a lot of speed under water."

Next they put on the belts that were weighted with lead. Hanging on each belt was a bag holding a knife with a cork handle.

"You won't always need the belt," the Professor said. "Most of the time the weight of the oxygen tank will keep you under water when you want to stay down. But sometimes you need one, and I thought you should get the feel of it under water."

With the belt on, Pete found he would settle to the bottom when he went under.

"Now let's get started on the best part of skin diving— using the oxygen tank." Professor Nevins reached into the boat and lifted out a tank about two and a half feet long, painted bright yellow. From the pointed end, two rubber tubes came out of the tank and ran to a rubber mouth piece. There was also a round knob set in the top of the tank. Pointing to it, Nevins said, "This controls the flow of air into the mouth piece. You can reach it over your shoulder when you are wearing the tank. That way, you can get more air, or less air, whichever you need."

He held the tank while Pete slipped his arms through the two canvas straps so that the tank hung on his back. Then the Professor looped the two rubber air tubes over Pete's head and handed Pete the mouth piece.

27

"Here, slip this into your mouth. You will find that you can hold it easily with your teeth. Even if you open your jaws a little, it won't fall out. The rubber front here covers your lips so no water can get into your mouth while you are breathing."

Pete slipped the mouth piece into his mouth and the Professor gave the handle one turn.

"Breathe in, Pete," he said. Then, "Are you getting enough oxygen?" Pete took several breaths and shook his his head that he was not.

The Professor gave it another turn. "How's that? Are you getting enough now?"

Pete nodded and pointed down at the water.

"All right, go ahead. Try it," the Professor said.

Pete went under. A moment later he came up, choking for air. The Professor burst out laughing.

"It's not funny." Pete said.

"Sure, it is. You wouldn't wait until I told you how to breathe."

Pete laughed too, this time. "I thought I knew how to breathe!"

"It is a little different with the tank. You have to pull in hard with your mouth, then blow the air out through your nose."

"Got it. Let me try it again."

Pete dived and this time he did it right.

For the next half hour Pete practiced. He went out into the harbor for a hundred yards under water, then came to the surface. The Professor made him practice going in a straight line.

"You have to swim with an even stroke, Pete. When you stay under longer, you want to know exactly where your boat is when you come up. If I am in town tomorrow," Professor Nevins went on, "I will pick up a couple of wrist compasses. Then we can practice doing some map problems under the water."

Pete thought how useful a compass could be. With it, a man could approach a boat under water without being seen. And when he learned to judge distance under water, he would be able to come up just where he wanted to.

On the way back to camp, Professor Nevins said, "This time the supper is on me."

After they had eaten and the sun was going down, Pete said, "I know everybody thinks I am off base, the way I feel about Fannin, but there is something fishy about that boat business of his. First of all, why didn't he rent space down near the main part of town where all the people are?"

"All right, Pete. That's one point."

"Next, why is he buzzing around the water in the middle of the night?"

"That is point two, provided it was Fannin."

"Third, what kind of business man making a start in a new town would treat me or any young fellow who was minding his own affairs the way he did me?"

The Professor nodded and Pete went on.

"Also, why hasn't he put any notices of his business plans in the paper?"

"Is that right?" the Professor asked.

"That's what my father said."

"That's odd, but not a full point against him. I can give you credit for only half on that one."

Pete took a deep breath. "And the fifth thing is the way he handled his boat yesterday when he came over for gas. He used it as if it were a car. No *real* boat man would do that. A car is a car and a boat is a boat. I don't think he knows enough about boats to tell the difference."

The Professor pulled on his pipe for a minute. Then he said, "I will go this far with you: taken all together, it looks odd. So the question is, what do you want to do about it?"

"Watch him."

"And you want me to help you?"

"Yes, if you will."

After another moment the Professor said, "I won't help you, Pete, but I will go with you if I have enough time. On one condition," he added, "that everything you do is completely within the law."

Later that evening, they moved silently around the curve of the beach, keeping the house boat in view. Lights were on. As they got closer, they stopped more often. They could hear voices but could not make out what was being said.

Pete and the Professor slid under the dock and sat on

the damp sand. The hull of the house boat was only a few feet from them.

The Professor whispered, "What are you expecting them to do, Pete?"

"I don't know," Pete whispered back.

At midnight the Professor pointed to his watch, then toward their tents. Pete nodded. When they were far enough away to speak in normal voices, Pete said, "You go on back to your camp. I am going to walk up to the top of the dune and take a look at the ocean."

Pete climbed slowly until he reached the top. There he sat down and stared out over the ocean. Far below him, the waves broke with a hissing roar on the beach, ran up the sand in a rush, and then slowly flowed back into the sea. As Pete leaned back, enjoying a sense of ease, something caught his eye far off to the right.

He stood and looked toward Lighthouse Point and could see the red and green light of a boat coming his way. At first it seemed to be heading straight for Main Inlet and he thought it was a fishing boat returning home. But it passed the inlet and kept coming toward him. Then a strange thing happened.

The lights suddenly went out.

Pete wondered what kind of fool would run at night without lights. Seconds passed . . . and then a full minute, before he saw the black shape again, drawing nearer. He could make it out quite clearly in the moonlight.

When it was directly opposite where he was standing,

Pete said to himself, "That's a PT boat, the kind that was used in the war!" He had seen too many of them at Hidden Harbor to make a mistake.

The PT boat kept on going. When it reached Sea Bird Island, three hundred yards off shore and in a direct line with the ocean side of shallow North Inlet, Pete heard the engines slow down.

A big anchor chain rattled down. After a moment it stopped. A man's voice carried across the water.

"All right, that's it!"

Pete watched for another fifteen minutes, but nothing more happened. Finally he could not stay quiet any longer. He had to tell Professor Nevins.

Getting up, he started back to the harbor. He turned to take one last look at the large black boat and got the surprise of his life.

A light was blinking from the pilot house of the PT boat. Pete ran back to a place where he could see the PT boat and still look down into the harbor.

Now there was a light blinking from the house boat!

Pete watched only a minute or so. Then he rushed down the beach. "Professor! Professor Nevins! Are you up?" he called when he reached the tent.

"Yes, Pete. What's the matter?"

Quickly, Pete explained. In less than five minutes they were back on the dune.

The blinking had stopped. In fact, there was nothing to show that a boat had been near Sea Bird Island.

They walked back slowly. As they stood in the moonlight, the Professor said. "Pete, are you sure you saw a PT boat blinking its lights?"

"I couldn't have dreamed up a boat that big. Honestly, Professor Nevins, you have to believe me," Pete protested.

CHAPTER THREE

Things Aren't Going
the Way I Expected

Pete woke up to find the Professor shaking him.

"Pete! Come on, snap out of it."

"I'm awake, I'm awake," Pete said. "What's the matter?" He crawled out into the gray light of dawn.

Professor Nevins came after him. In the early sunrise the air was still chill.

The Professor looked worried and angry.

"I woke up early," he said, "and decided to take a walk along the shore. Half way to the house boat I saw that all the marsh grass just a few yards off the beach had been stamped down. I took off my sneakers and waded into the water because there was something familiar about that spot. When I got there I found two of my nesting boxes—all broken up. They were lying right in the middle of the grass, and the eggs were scattered and broken. I could see the remains of the shells."

"Do you think it was Fannin?"

"That's the first thing I thought. Then it struck me that I was blaming him without proof—just what I told you not to do. So I tried to figure out who else might want to wreck those boxes. They have no value. No one would want to steal them. They were just smashed up and left lying there.

"I thought it might have been kids. You know how children sometimes destroy things for no reason at all. Then it occurred to me that Fannin and Bucko had seen me checking those boxes yesterday afternoon while they were working on the dock."

"But when could they have done it? We were around here all day."

"After we went to bed," Professor Nevins replied.

"The question is *why?*" Pete said. After a pause, he added, "I have one idea. Fannin broke up the boxes because he wants you away from this end of the harbor."

"But I am not doing anything to them!" the Professor said.

"You are doing one thing just by being here," Pete said. "You are where you can see everything they do. Don't forget, your camp is much closer to the factory than mine is. Whatever they are planning, they can't carry it through until they are rid of you."

Professor Nevins nodded. "That makes sense."

"Why do *you* think they did it?" Pete asked.

"Well," Professor Nevins said, "first I asked myself, *why in the middle of the night?*"

"I know!" Pete almost shouted. "Because of the PT boat! Because of the boat signals."

"While I was walking over here I thought of something else." Professor Nevins looked at Pete. "Do you think they might have seen you up there on the hill?"

Pete remembered the bright moonlight. "Boy, what a dope I am." He shook his head sadly. "I just stood there like a statue."

"Don't worry about it," Professor Nevins assured him. "If they saw you, there's nothing we can do about it."

Pete began to make a fire for breakfast.

"Are you going to town today?" Nevins asked.

Pete nodded. "I told Dad I'd check in at the yard this morning. Why?"

"As long as you are going to the yard, could you pick up those wrist compasses in town for me? You can be back by lunch time."

"Why not?" Pete agreed. "Skin diving with a compass sounds great. The sooner we begin, the better."

They cleaned up around the fire. Pete waded out to his boat and began raising his sails. In minutes, he was on his way across the harbor toward the boat yard under a good breeze.

When Pete lowered his sails and drifted in toward the

36

Professor's camp three hours later, he had a leather case holding a pair of powerful field glasses hanging around his neck.

Professor Nevins came down to the edge of the water to help Pete pull the bow up on the beach.

"I brought these along," Pete said, holding up the glasses. "I thought in case you had any doubts about that PT boat, you could see for yourself."

"I have to check any nests that may be left, Pete. Your word for the boat will be good enough with me."

"I will take a look anyway," Pete replied. "I won't be gone more than an hour. Are you going to put up new boxes for the birds?"

"Perhaps in the fall, so that they will weather over the winter."

At two-thirty, Pete took the field glasses and started toward Lighthouse Point. A few hundred yards down the beach, he climbed the dunes. When he reached the top, he settled himself, swung around in the sand and trained his field glasses on the water near Sea Bird Island. Just as he was sure it would be, a PT lay quietly at anchor. The glasses brought the boat so close that he could see three men sitting on the deck near the stern. They were smoking and talking, and it was clear to Pete that they had no work to do. They seemed to be just sitting around, waiting.

Getting to his feet, Pete started back to camp. He found Nevins working over his charts and papers.

"Anything happen?" the Professor asked.

"The PT boat was there, all right," Pete said, and told what he had seen.

"I think it's time I got a look for myself," the Professor said.

Together he and Pete went back to the ocean side of the Dunes. Standing in water up to their knees about a quarter of a mile from the house boat, looking out at the PT boat, the Professor spoke quietly.

"Pete, take a quick look back at the house boat."

Pete looked out of the corner of his eye and said, "Someone is up in the wheel house watching us."

"I thought so."

At ten o'clock that night they were sitting under the factory dock, only a few yards from the house boat. Again, the moon was shining brightly.

Pete leaned close to the Professor's ear and whispered softly, "If I move closer to the boat, I may be able to hear what they are talking about."

As quietly as he could, Pete got up and started down toward the edge of the water. He walked into the water a few feet. He could hear men's voices inside the house boat, but he could not make out what was being said.

He began moving down along the side of the house boat, between it and the dock. At last he came directly

under a window. He heard a noise, as if someone had stood up. The window over his head opened and he heard Bucko's voice clearly.

"All right, then," Bucko said, "if that's what you want." He sounded angry. "But I tell you, it's not a good idea in the middle of the night."

Fannin's voice came down to Pete.

"You let me be the judge of that, Bucko. Now that the boat is here, we have to speed up our work. Things are not going as I expected."

Bucko did not answer.

The next instant, Pete nearly jumped out of his skin as a loud hammering started inside the hull, right next to his ear. He had to fight down the urge to run.

The pounding continued for half a minute while Pete stood with his hands pressed against the side of the house boat. He did not know what the sound meant and wondered if he should get out of there.

A moment later Pete had something more to worry about. The hammering stopped, and he heard the heavy sound of a truck approaching the factory along Shore Road. As he listened, it turned into the factory grounds. Over his head, he heard a door open.

"Hold it, Bucko!" Fannin said. "The truck is here!"

Fannin and Bucko came running up on deck, and a shaft of light shot down between the house boat and and dock, directly on Pete. He ducked back under the dock as feet pounded over his head.

As quickly as he could, he moved back to where the Professor was waiting.

"What is that truck doing?" Pete whispered.

As Pete and the Professor watched, lights came on in the factory and the truck backed up to the loading platform. Two men got out. Fannin and Bucko joined them, and the four began to take crates from the truck into the factory.

Suddenly, they were done. The truck drove back out of the factory grounds. In a moment, everything was silent.

Pete said, "I sure would like to see what is in those crates. Let's slip around and get up close to the factory." In five minutes they were at the rear of the factory.

"Look at this!" Professor Nevins whispered.

A ladder was standing against the factory wall, right under a window.

"That's our chance," Pete said.

The Professor shook his head. "No, too much of a risk."

"I won't go inside, don't worry," Pete answered. Without waiting, he began to climb.

From the top, Pete was just able to lift his head above the sill. Looking down, he glimpsed two men. From their size and shape, he felt sure they were Fannin and Bucko. There was only one dim light directly over their heads, hanging on a long cord from the ceiling. It cast deep shadows all around the room.

As Pete watched, the larger of the men reached into

the crate and lifted out a long object, wrapped in tar paper. Slowly he pulled off the paper and held up the object.

In an instant Pete was down next to the Professor.

"Rifles!" he whispered. "There are rifles in those crates!"

The Professor took Pete by the arm and pulled him away. They started back toward the Dunes.

CHAPTER FOUR

We Have to Be Smarter

When Pete and the Professor were safely away, Pete stopped.

"That proves it!"

"Hold on a minute, Pete!" The Professor started walking. "This is not a game. How do you know that those are not legal guns?"

"But Fannin is supposed to be in the *boat* business!" Pete protested.

Turning to Pete, Professor Nevins said, "Those rifles are probably part of Fannin's business. He may be going into the sporting goods business. Don't forget, there is lots of hunting around here in the fall."

"Look, Professor," Pete argued. "You have as many doubts about Fannin as I have."

"Even if I did, Pete, I would want to handle this thing correctly. In the morning, you go see your father. Have him find out if Fannin has a permit to handle guns. He must know someone at Town Hall who would answer a question like that for him without asking too many questions in return."

"I—I guess that's the best way," Pete answered slowly. "So we wait until morning, right?"

"Right," Pete agreed. They walked on to Pete's tent. Pete saluted good night and stepped inside, curled up in his sleeping bag, and fell asleep.

Pete walked in the back door of the Dana house the next morning just as his father was pouring a cup of coffee. Wesley Dana looked up and smiled.

"Hello, Pete! What are you doing here?"

"Hi, Dad," Pete said. "Wanted to talk to you about something."

"Well, have some breakfast first," his father said.

Pete walked over to the stove and poured himself a cup of coffee. "Dad," he said, "I'd better begin at the beginning. Have you time to listen to the whole story?"

"Sure, Pete, go ahead."

Pete told his father about losing his sailboat, the speed boats in the night, Professor Nevins' broken nesting boxes, the arrival of the PT boat, the blinking signals and, finally, the rifles he had seen.

Mr. Dana sat silent for a while, thinking and staring

out the window. When he spoke, his tone was very earnest.

"Now, Pete, what you have told me is pretty serious. If you are wrong, you could get into a lot of trouble making a false statement."

"I know what I saw, Dad, and I saw rifles."

"All right, but let's start again at the beginning. First of all, you got off to a bad start with Fannin. You told me yourself that you didn't like him."

"I know, Dad, but what about my boat being cut loose?"

"You believe it was cut loose. But you admitted the rope looked worn through. I am just wondering, son, if you are blaming Fannin for your careless tying of the knot."

"I know how I tied that knot, Dad! And I know there was nothing for the line to rub against. But, all right, what about the rest of the things?"

"You say Fannin is running his boats at night. I say you do not really know who it is. But even if it is Fannin, what of it? You would not test boats at night, but maybe Fannin would. Just because you can't see a good reason does not mean he doesn't have one."

"How about the PT boat?"

Mr. Dana shook his head. "I believe there is a PT boat out by Sea Bird Island, if you say so. But you are only guessing that it has anything to do with Fannin."

"But what about the blinking signals, Dad?"

45

"I don't know," Mr. Dana answered slowly. "Are you sure they were signals? You know Morse code. Were they sending words you could read?"

"Of course not!" Pete answered, as if his father should know better. "They were sending in some other code."

"Oh, come on, Pete. This is not the movies, this is real life! How do you know they were even signaling to each other?"

Pete shook his head. "Boy, this is crazy! I am losing this argument, but I know I am right!" He looked straight into his father's eyes. "Dad, you gave a neat explanation of everything else, but what about the rifles? Was I just seeing things?"

Wesley Dana was silent for several moments. Then he spoke. "No, Pete, probably not. That's something that puzzles me. The difference is this. You believe all the other things are proof that Fannin is doing something against the law. I don't. So naturally, you think the rifles are the last piece of evidence in a perfect case against him. However, the rifles are the *only* thing that really makes me wonder."

"Then you will do something about it?" Pete urged.

"I will make some telephone calls, as you suggest. Right now, you can do something for me, too. Finish stacking the lumber over in the yard."

Pete went to work with a will, stacking the lumber according to size. Soon he was more than half finished.

"Hey, Pete! Come here!" his father called.

Pete threw a heavy piece of lumber on the pile and ran for the house.

"What did you find out?" he asked as he ran in to the kitchen.

"Sit down. Take it easy," his father said. "First of all, I found out that Fannin does not have a gun permit. So if you really saw crates of rifles, maybe something odd *is* going on."

"I did see them!" Pete said.

"All right, take it easy, Pete," Wesley Dana said. "Next, I called the Police Chief. You know I am pretty friendly with John Simmons. I asked him what he knew about Fannin. He told me not much. He only talked to Fannin once shortly after Fannin had first arrived in town."

"Is the Chief going to do anything?"

"Yes. He said he would go to the factory this afternoon."

Pete got up and walked over to the window. He saw
Nick down near the dock. "Will the Chief call you?"

"Yes, when he gets back."

"Mind if I stick around and help Nick out?" Pete
suggested.

"Sure, son. He is behind on a job as it is."

Pete walked down through the yard. Nick smiled as
he approached.

"How are you making out?"

"You won't laugh when you hear what I have to tell
you," Pete said.

When he had told Nick about the factory, Nick raised
his eyebrows in surprise.

"I told Dad I would help you until the Chief gets
back from the factory. What do we have to do?"

"Finish stacking this lumber," Nick said, "and then
put those props away."

Now time passed slowly. Pete tried to keep his mind
on his work, but he kept wondering what the Chief
was doing. Finally, he heard his father calling from the
back porch.

Pete ran up through the yard and took the porch steps
three at a time.

"Any news? What happened?" he asked his father.

"No news," Wesley Dana said. "I just called you up here for lunch. I made a batch of sandwiches."

Pete could not hide his disappointment.

"Look, Pete," Mr. Dana told him, "you are not a kid any more. Be patient. If you can't wait things out you won't be much help in the yard."

"I know that, Dad," Pete said.

"Well, you don't exactly show it. You seem to want to act first and think second. When people grow older, they like to make sure they are doing the right thing before they start anything." Mr. Dana went to the icebox for a bottle of milk. "Nobody can afford to make too many mistakes."

"Isn't it better sometimes to plunge right in and get the job done?"

"It won't work in a boat yard, Pete, any more than it will anywhere else in life. For instance, if you give a boat owner an estimate on a job without thinking it out and have to do half the work over, you can't charge him for the extra time. You have to stick to your price and take the loss yourself."

Pete did not speak. He knew that what his father said was true. They ate their sandwiches in silence.

"Well, better get back to work," Pete said, and walked out into the yard again.

It was the middle of the afternoon when Wesley Dana walked slowly through the yard. Pete took one look at his father and knew that something had gone wrong.

"What happened, Dad?" he asked.

Wesley Dana's voice was flat and deep.

"The Chief says that, when he drove over, Fannin was alone. Fannin seemed surprised. Then, when the Chief asked if he could look around, Fannin got angry. He asked if the Chief were looking for anything in particular. The Chief said no, it just was a friendly visit. Fannin said it did not look very friendly."

Pete was scared. "That was just a bluff."

"Anyway, the Chief went into the factory and, Pete, he told me *he did not see a thing!* He said it was empty from end to end. It has concrete floors and no basement. The only thing the Chief saw was one of Fannin's red boats down at the end near the dock. And some tools.

"The Chief walked all around the factory. He looked in the woods behind it. He looked under the dock on the sand. And then, when he was about to leave, Fannin did something he did not expect at all."

"What?" Pete asked.

"Fannin asked the Chief to have a look aboard the house boat, too. He told the Chief that, if he was going to be suspected of something and the Chief did not even tell him what it was, he had to clear his name. So he *demanded* that the Chief search the house boat."

"I can tell what's coming," Pete put in. "He didn't find a thing."

"That's right. He went over that house boat from one end to the other. He told me that the best thing we can do is just forget the whole thing. And Pete, whatever you do, he said not to go near Fannin or the house boat again. Leave him alone. Do not bother him or say anything to him."

Pete thought he had never been more disappointed. "All right," he said. "I guess that settles it." He untied his sailboat from the end of the gas float, stepped into it and pushed off.

His father followed him to the end of the float. "Pete, don't get the idea I am blaming you."

Pete waved without speaking. He was too mixed up to trust himself to say anything more. As he steered the boat back toward the Dunes, he went over a whole series of questions in his mind.

What had happened? Why had the Chief not found any rifles? Could he have been wrong? He had been so sure he had seen them. Then where did they go? The Chief had searched the woods, the factory, the dock, and the house boat. Could they have been taken away again, by truck, during the night? But that did not make sense.

When he got back to the Dunes, Pete told the entire story to Professor Nevins. They watched the sun go down and the moon come up—still talking about the mystery.

It was an hour after darkness when they heard the familiar sound of one of Fannin's boats. The engine came to life with a roar, ran slowly for a few minutes, and then became louder as it moved away from the factory.

For the first time since they had heard a boat moving around the harbor at night, it seemed to be heading their way.

"What do you make of that?" the Professor asked.

"Maybe they are trying to see if we are here," Pete suggested.

They stopped talking and listened.

The boat engine grew louder and louder. As it came nearer, they realized it was headed for North Inlet.

Then, suddenly, the engine noise almost stopped.

"I know!" Pete cried. "They went out through North Inlet! They are heading for the PT boat."

"Maybe you are right, Pete! Come on, let's go! We can wait by the inlet and see if they come back that way."

In a few minutes they had reached North Inlet and flopped down behind the sand dunes next to the winding channel of water flowing from the ocean into the harbor.

Fifteen minutes later, they heard the engine again. It was coming from the ocean.

"That's it!" Pete said. "We were right!"

A moment later the speed boat shot past them and was gone. When it reached the factory, the engine stopped. Then, a moment or two later, the lights in the house boat went on.

"Do you think what I think?" Pete asked.

Slowly, the Professor nodded. "But, Pete, where were the rifles this noon when the Chief searched the factory?"

Pete shook his head. "That is the big question! And we don't have the answer."

"Who would think of operating a gun-running ring from a little harbor in New England?" the Professor said, half to himself.

"Pretty smart," Pete agreed. "And somehow, we have to be smarter."

They walked slowly back to the Professor's camp.

CHAPTER FIVE

We Need Action, Not Talk

Just before noon the next day, Pete took the field glasses and walked down the beach. When he was half way to Lighthouse Point, he climbed the highest dune. Taking the glasses out of their leather case, he trained them on the Town Dock. It was over three miles across the harbor, but with the glasses he could see the flag pole clearly.

"Thought so," he said aloud to himself. "Storm signals." All morning, Pete had watched gray clouds piling up.

Now Pete turned and faced the ocean. For several minutes he watched the clouds grow darker. The sea was beginning to get rough. White foam appeared on the waves and Pete thought of the PT boat.

He looked through the glasses and saw that it was

rolling in the water. "Have fun, boys," he said to himself. "If you are not used to boats, you are going to have quite a time before today is over." He got up and started back to his camp. When he got there the Professor was waiting for him.

"You missed something, Pete. While you were gone, another truck came in and delivered more crates to the factory."

"In broad daylight?"

The Professor nodded.

"Since the Chief was there yesterday, Fannin is probably sure he can do just about anything he wants." Pete somehow felt tricked. "But I know one thing they won't do," he added.

"What's that?"

"They won't be going out to the PT boat tonight. If they try it, they will be swamped. It is going to be rough out there a little later—*really* rough!"

After a moment, Pete went on. "As a matter of fact, I think we ought to put some logs around the sides of our tents. We might as well be prepared for a real blow."

In the next hour they cooked a hot lunch, made a pack of sandwiches to eat in the evening, and put logs and heavy timbers from the beach all around the edges of both tents.

"Do you think they will hold?" Professor Nevins looked worried. "You know, all my records and instruments are here with me. Perhaps I should take them across the harbor to your house now, before the big storm begins."

Pete looked out and then up at the sky. "Too late," he said. "The wind is too strong already."

In less than ten minutes, the first patter of rain drops hit the tent. A moment later, a bolt of lightning flashed across the sky, lighting the whole harbor as if a very strong bulb had been flashed on for just an instant. Deep thunder rumbled in the distance.

"Oh, boy," Pete said. "This is going to be a real one. Let's get our foul-weather gear. Then we will be ready for anything that happens." He began running for his tent down the beach.

By the time he got back, the rain was pouring down.

It became damp inside the tent. Pete noticed little drops forming along the tent edges. As the rain stopped for a moment, they heard a stir in the air that sounded like a long sigh.

"Here she comes," Pete said out loud. "The wind, I mean."

At first, the wind blew in gusts, tugging strongly at the tent, then letting up. Soon it was blowing without stopping.

"Will the tent hold?" the Professor asked.

"Maybe, maybe not." Pete shook his head.

"Pete, I can't let those instruments be ruined," Professor Nevins told him. "They belong to the University. It would cost me a small fortune for new ones. I must get them to your house some way."

"Okay," Pete agreed. "Where is your station wagon?"

"Parked off by the side of the road near the old air field down past the factory."

"All right," Pete stood up. "Let's go."

"Thanks, Pete." Professor Nevins walked over to the instruments and began wrapping them in heavy oil skins. "Be ready in a minute."

After the instruments were packed, it took Pete and Professor Nevins nearly an hour to reach the thin pine woods that curved around the back of the factory. As they plodded slowly through the trees, with small streams of water running down through the carpet of pine needles toward the harbor, Pete suddenly stopped.

"What is it?" he asked.

"Look at that," Pete said, and pointed ahead.

In among some bushes lay a large box, covered with pine branches. They walked closer and Pete threw off some of the branches.

The large object was a crate—just like the ones Pete had seen through the factory window.

"Today's delivery," the Professor said. "That gives me an idea, Pete. You said they couldn't get these guns out to the PT boat tonight?"

"That's right."

"Then why not bring your father over here? We can bring the instruments to your house and drive your father back here. Let him see the guns for himself."

"Great!" Pete exclaimed. "You know, Dad said he

did believe me about the guns. But if he saw them with his own eyes . . ."

It was early evening when they had safely stowed the instruments in the station wagon. The wind continued to blow in force.

"Hope the car starts," the Professor muttered. It did, on the third try.

It was slow driving in the wind and rain. Branches had blown down, and the road was made slippery by wet leaves. Neither one spoke as they drove along. Then the lights of a car appeared in front of them.

As the other car shot by in a shower of splashing water, Pete grabbed the Professor's arm.

"Hey, I think that was our boat yard truck!"

"Are you sure?"

"I only got a quick look, but I am pretty sure."

"But where would they be going?"

"I don't know," Pete said.

"Let's keep on, Pete. We can't be sure it was your father or Nick."

In another ten minutes they had reached Pete's house. There was a note on the door. It said:

Pete: In case you come home for any reason, I am at the factory. Rush call from Fannin. House boat breaking loose.— Must hurry. Dad

Pete whistled. "Come on, let's go."

As quickly as possible, they carried Professor Nevin's instruments from the station wagon into the house and got back into the car. The drive back seemed to Pete to be at a snail's pace. At last the Professor had parked and they were again walking through the pines toward the factory.

Five minutes later the path began curving toward the harbor. Up ahead, someone had turned on the two factory lights that were set high on the end of the building. It was a scene of wild confusion. The house boat was going up and down like a roller coaster. Pete saw instantly that only one end was still tied to the dock. In the light, four figures were running back and forth.

Pete raced to the end of the dock and ran up to his father. The house boat was about ten yards from the edge of the dock, rolling in the high waves. Wesley Dana had a heavy rope in his hand. One end had a large loop in it and Mr. Dana was trying to throw it across the open water on to a low, heavy iron post set in one corner of the house boat deck. He swung and then threw the rope like a lasso. It flew out and landed on the deck. But it missed the post and slipped off, falling into the water with a splash.

Pete called to his father. He looked tired, and the rain had plastered his hair to his head.

"Glad you got here, Pete," his father said. "We have had a rough time. Only one line on the house boat when we got here. We got one new one on her, but I am having the devil's own time getting another one on. We have to get a couple more lines on this end. Then we

60

have to haul the other end of that boat in to the dock."

"Won't she ride out the storm the way she is?"

Mr. Dana shook his head. "Probably, but Fannin insists that we bring the other end in to the dock. Says it won't be safe otherwise. He's paying the bill, so what he says goes."

Pete looked at the house boat, crashing up and down in the white water.

"I can go out hand over hand on one of the ropes, Dad. When I get on the deck, you can throw me some lines. I will make them fast to the far side of the boat. Then we can all haul the other end of the boat back to the dock."

Wesley Dana did not answer immediately. Finally he spoke.

"I want to give this rope one more toss, Pete."

His father turned and threw the heavy line with all his might. It flew out, landed on the edge of the house boat deck—and fell off again.

Pete walked toward the other end of the dock. He found Nick wrapping cloth around the heavy rope that ran out to the house boat.

"How are they holding out?" he asked Nick.

Nick grunted and looked up.

"Oh, hello, Pete. They aren't doing so good. These lines are all right for a calm day, but they are not strong enough for stormy weather."

He looked up and down the dock. Pete did the same.

The Professor was talking to Fannin at the very end of the dock. Bucko was walking swiftly up toward the factory. Nick leaned closer to Pete.

"Tell you the truth, Pete," he said, "whoever put these lines on her doesn't know the first thing about tying up a boat. Another funny thing," Nick went on, "when we got here, things were worse than now. There was only one line on the house boat and Fannin was just standing there. Well, your father picked up a rope and tied a loop in it. On his second try, he caught a post on the boat. That took the strain off this line. Otherwise this baby would be heading across the harbor right now. With the wind and the tide, she would drive right on through our boats and go up on shore."

"You mean they weren't doing *anything?*" Pete asked.

"I don't think they knew how or what to do," Nick said. "But that's not the only funny thing. As soon as we got the new line on her, Fannin walks up and says to your father, 'Mister Dana, we have to get the other end of the house boat in against the dock.'"

"What did Dad say?"

"He said, 'Sure thing, Mister Fannin. Soon as this wind lets up a little bit, we will do just that.'"

"And what did Fannin say?"

"He asked when your father thought the wind would let up. Your father told him along about dawn. And then Fannin said, 'That won't be soon enough. We *have* to get it against the dock now.'"

62

"But why?" Pete asked. "What difference does it make? If we can get a couple more lines on this end, she'll be safe. Why kill ourselves getting the other end in when we can do it just as easily in the . . ."

Pete stopped talking as Fannin walked past him, headed for Wesley Dana. Nick stood up from the rope he had finished wrapping.

"There!" he said. "That won't wear through for a while."

"Here comes Bucko with more rope," Pete said.

Bucko walked slowly on to the dock carrying a huge coil of new rope. He took it to where Fannin and Wesley Dana were talking and dumped it on the dock. As Pete and Nick watched, Wesley Dana nodded at something Fannin said and walked over to them.

"All right, Pete," he said, wiping the rain out of his eyes. "You are going to get your chance to be a hero. Fannin insists we get the other end in to the dock, so I am going to let you try to make it out there. I know you are a monkey when it comes to climbing, and that is the only chance we have."

"I hate to do it for *him*," Pete said, nodding toward Fannin. "But I'll try it to save the boat."

In spite of the wind, rain and waves, Pete knew he had the strength to pull himself hand over hand out to the house boat. Nick, Pete and his father walked over to the new rope. Nick picked up a short piece of line and handed it to Pete.

"Here," he said, "put this around your waist, and tie yourself to the heavy line. Then if you get tired and stop to rest, you won't fall in the water."

Pete looped the rope around his waist twice and sat on the edge of the dock. Then he tied the ends of the rope from his waist to the heavy line running out to the house boat.

"Here goes," he said. Pete shoved himself off the end of the dock and began to pull himself hand over hand out to the house boat. The five men stood on the edge of the dock, watching.

Suddenly, a wave carried the house boat several feet

back toward the dock. The line went slack and Pete dropped down with it. He felt the water close over his head, but it was only a moment before he was back above the surface, the heavy rope tight again.

"You all right?" he heard Nick shout.

"Sure!" Pete called back.

Half the way across, Pete found that he was tiring. He had not realized how heavy his foul-weather clothing would be. Besides that, he was now carrying a load of water in his clothes from the wave that had washed over him. He paused for a few seconds to catch his breath, letting his weight fall on the rope around his waist. Silently, he thanked Nick's quick thinking in suggesting the safety line.

As he swung around on the rope, he saw Nick and Bucko getting the new lines ready. With an effort, he hauled himself the remaining few yards until he could touch the deck of the house boat. When he got both hands on it, he pulled himself up on the deck.

He stood up and waved.

A moment later the first rope whistled on to the deck and Pete grabbed it before it could skid off.

"All set here," he shouted.

Pete pulled the rope along the side deck. When he reached the far end, out in the harbor, it was much darker. The lights on the end of the factory just reached him. It took Pete a long time to get the rope well secured, but he wanted to make sure he tied good knots.

Then he came back for the second line. This time it was easy, and in less than two minutes he was ready to start back to the dock.

Pete made the return trip without trouble. As he came within reach of the dock, several pairs of hands caught hold of him and pulled him to safety.

"Great job, Pete!" Nick said.

Now they started pulling the house boat in to the dock. With the new ropes on the far end it was easy. Each time the house boat came toward them a little bit, they held it there by taking up the slack in the new lines which were wound around the posts that supported the dock. Finally, the side of the house boat was resting against the length of the dock from which it had broken loose hours before.

It was only then that Pete noticed the Professor was no longer with them.

"Where did Professor Nevins go?" he asked Nick.

"He was worried about his tent, so he decided to go over and check on it. I told him we could handle this without him."

"Why don't you go over, Pete?" Nick said, "We can finish this now."

"All right, maybe I will," Pete said.

"Sure, Pete," his father told him. "And Pete . . . I'm glad you got here. This was one time when we needed action, not talk—and you supplied it."

Pete smiled and started off. He found the strong winds

had knocked down one end of the tent. But a half hour of work, using more rope and heavy pieces of wood, secured the tent again.

"There," Pete said. "That should stand in anything, no matter how bad."

"Let's get inside and peel off these wet clothes," the Professor said. "And why don't you sleep here tonight? There is plenty of room."

Pete suddenly realized he was worn out. The thought of crawling right into bed sounded great.

"Yes, sir!" he sighed.

He got out of his wet clothes. The Professor turned off the battery lamp. Pete slipped into the sleeping bag and sighed. Suddenly he was sitting upright.

"Professor Nevins," Pete exclaimed, "we never told Dad and Nick anything about the guns!"

"So we didn't, Pete." The Professor too sat upright. They looked across at each other.

CHAPTER SIX

The Proof We Were
Looking For

Pete dreamed that he was alone in a huge, dark room. In the empty darkness someone kept calling him. He tried to shout that he was coming, but he had no voice.

"Pete! Hey, Pete! Are you in there?"

It was Nick's voice, calling from somewhere outside. Pete threw off the covers and dashed out of Professor Nevins' tent.

The work boat from the yard was a few yards off the beach. Nick was standing on the deck with his hands cupped around his mouth. With a sweep of his arm he motioned for Pete to come out.

Something was wrong, that was clear. Pete waded into the water and headed out to Nick.

"What's the matter?" he asked, beside the boat.

"Your father was hurt last night, after you left," Nick called.

"What happened?" Pete's face went white.

"He's all right now," Nick said. "Somehow he got his foot caught between the house boat and the dock. Just then a wave shoved the house boat in—and it broke his leg. I got him to the hospital in the truck."

"How is he now?"

"He was sleeping when I went over there this morning. They set his leg last night. The doctor told me I could bring you in early in the afternoon."

Pete was silent for a moment. "If Fannin and Bucko had not been so stupid about tying up that house boat, this never would have happened," he exploded.

"It was an accident, Pete, that's all."

Pete sighed. "Everything was going fine around here until Fannin showed up."

"Forget about it," Nick said. "Swim back, get your clothes on and go around to the factory dock. I will pick you up there."

"All right." Pete headed back toward the beach. Without waking the Professor, he dressed quickly and started around the curve of the beach toward the factory dock.

Pete looked curiously at the house boat. Neither Fannin nor Bucko was around. Everything was quiet. It was a perfect day. Pete found it hard to believe that, only twelve hours before, they had been battling to save the big house boat in a wild storm.

"Let's go to the house first," Pete said to Nick, "before we go to the hospital."

Nick nodded, gunned the engine and swung the boat around. Pete stood next to him in the pilot house as they churned across the harbor.

Finally he said, "Nick, why do you think Fannin insisted we get the other end of the house boat into the dock right in the middle of the storm?"

"I guess he was afraid that if we had only the one end tied it would break loose and be wrecked."

"But you and Dad both told him it would be all right to wait a few hours—until the wind died down."

"I know, but some people are like that. They have to do things the way *they* want them."

"No, I think there was more to it than that. The Professor and I found another crate of rifles yesterday—up in the woods behind the factory."

Nick gave a long, low whistle.

"That's right. We were on the way to the house when you and Dad passed in the truck. When we got to the house, I found the note and we rushed right back."

"And you never showed the rifles to your father?"

"We didn't have time."

Nick nodded. "But if there really are guns there, why didn't Chief Simmons find them when he looked around?"

"I think Fannin has some secret space in the house boat. That would explain why he wanted both ends back against the dock."

70

"I doubt it," Nick said. "It is hard to build a secret hiding place in a boat."

They were approaching the boat yard dock. Pete went out on to the forward deck and picked up one of the lines. He stood in the bow as Nick reduced speed and guided the boat into the small dock. They walked together toward the Dana house.

When Pete had washed and put on a clean shirt, they got into Nick's car and drove along Shore Road to town. Nick parked across the street from the hospital and the two of them walked up the steps and inside.

After a few minutes, Pete found Doctor Spence.

"Your father is all right now," the doctor told him, "so don't worry. I went in to see him a few minutes ago. Come on, let's go up."

Wesley Dana's room was clean and white, and Pete felt as though he should speak in a whisper. The shades were down but Wesley Dana was awake, propped up with two pillows behind his head.

"Hi, Dad, are you all right?" Pete asked, walking over to the bed.

Wesley Dana smiled. "Sure, Pete, I'm fine."

"Anything I can do for you, Wesley?" Doctor Spence asked.

"Not a thing, Doc, except tell me when I can get out of here."

The doctor frowned. "Listen, Wes, this is not the boat yard. I give the orders around here. First of all, you are going to stay in bed here for three more days. Then, when I do let you go home, you are going to stay off your feet for another week. After that I may give you a pair of crutches. Now that's orders."

"All right, all right," Wesley Dana said.

"You have Nick and Pete to look after things. You are going to be an easy-chair boss for at least two months," the doctor finished in a firm voice. He waved to Pete and Nick and walked out of the room.

"Well, Dad, my camping trip is over," Pete said.

"I'm afraid so, Pete. You and Nick are going to be pretty busy the rest of the summer."

"Don't worry about the yard. We can handle things until you are up and around again."

"I am sure you can," Pete's father smiled at him. "I just wish your vacation hadn't been spoiled."

"Forget that," Pete said. "There is just one thing, Dad. Can I wait until tomorrow to move back?"

"Sure, Pete," Wesley Dana said. His voice sounded tired. Nick took Pete by the arm.

"I think we ought to be going," Nick said. "You look as if you could do with a nap, Wes."

"Guess I could," Wesley Dana said in a sleepy voice.

"Be back tomorrow, Dad," Pete told him. He and Nick quietly left the room.

That evening, Nick, Pete and the Professor sat together around the Professor's camp fire. They had eaten and were talking about the house boat and last night's storm.

Pete stood up and stretched. "I guess I will watch the house boat for a while. Maybe something will happen."

Nick got up. "If I don't get home soon, my wife will think I have shipped out to sea. See you tomorrow, Pete. Good night, Professor Nevins."

Pete rowed Nick out to the work boat, then returned to shore. He sat down next to Nevins.

"I know!" Pete snapped his fingers. "I can watch the house boat from the water."

The Professor looked troubled. "I don't know, Pete. I don't like the sound of it."

"I will only be a few yards from shore," Pete explained. "I can get out of the water and back here quicker than they can come by boat."

"I guess you know what you're doing, Pete, but don't move out of here until after dark."

Pete smiled. "Aye, aye, sir."

"Another thing. I don't care what you see or hear, *do not go aboard that house boat!*"

"I don't see how we are ever going to get anything on Fannin that way," Pete objected.

"Pete, it is not your business to go aboard the house boat. If anyone goes, it should be the police."

Pete grinned. "All right. I will keep that in mind."

At ten-thirty that night, Pete slipped into the water just

below the Professor's tent. He was wearing his bathing trunks and a dark shirt. Wading quietly, Pete followed the curve of the beach as it led around to the factory. He remembered a spot not too far from the house boat where the marsh grass was heavy. He would watch from there, he decided, and settled down to wait.

Standing still in the water, Pete began to feel a chill. A breeze was blowing and the water felt cold. He began to shiver. "All this is Fannin's fault," he thought. "Everything was fine in Hidden Harbor until Fannin came along. Now everything is changed."

His father was in the hospital with a broken leg. He and Nick would be doing the work of three men for the rest of the summer. Worst of all, Fannin was pushing everyone around and no one seemed able to do anything about it.

Pete was shivering so hard he knew he would have to move soon. He decided to go around to the other end of the house boat. From where he was, Pete could see no lights. He decided it was safer to be wet and cold than caught on the beach. He waded out into the harbor until he could no longer stand, then began to swim as quietly as he could.

Half way around the boat, Pete saw lights in the forward cabin. A door opened. A shaft of light from the door cut across the open water. Pete took a deep breath and ducked under. He swam as far as he could and then came up quietly. With a sigh of relief he saw that he was past the light beam. Then he heard Fannin's voice.

"Let's find out if they are ready," Fannin said.

The door slammed shut. Pete rolled over on his back, keeping his eyes on the house boat. In the moonlight he saw Fannin and Bucko climb to the upper deck and go into the pilot house. Pete was now far enough past to head in toward shore. When his feet touched bottom, he began wading until he found a new place in the high grass.

Suddenly, the light in the pilot house flashed out toward North Inlet. Pete's heart began to pound. "That's it!" he thought. They were going to make another run tonight. He couldn't see whether there was a return signal from the PT boat, but perhaps Professor Nevins had been watching. The Professor! They would see him if he were sitting on top of the hill.

Half a minute later, the signal stopped. There was silence for several minutes as Pete stood in the water, shivering in his soaking wet shirt.

Then the sound of a motor boat engine broke the silence of the night. Pete guessed that Fannin and Bucko had come down from the pilot house and along the dock to the speed boat without using any light.

Pete spotted the boat as it shot away from the dock. Cutting in a wide circle, it headed for North Inlet.

Without thinking what he was doing, he began to wade closer. He was surprised, a moment later, to find himself touching the house boat. A ladder hung down the out-

side, facing the harbor. He waded around to it and reached up for the first step.

Only then did Pete remember that Professor Nevins had told him not to go aboard. He took his hand off the step and stood there, unable to decide what to do.

"Everyone keeps telling me to stay away from Fannin," he told himself. "How can I ever get proof that way?"

It seemed to Pete that now was his one chance to find the thing everyone else had missed. He did not have to stay long—just a few minutes. He would be able to hear Fannin and Bucko as soon as they came back through North Inlet. He could get off the house boat in plenty of time to get away.

Without thinking about it any more, Pete started up the ladder. Reaching the deck, he stopped to listen. All was quiet. He walked softly toward the door just ahead of him. Peering through the window next to the door, Pete saw the dim shapes of furniture inside. He was surprised to see that the main cabin was set down in the hull of the house boat.

Opening the door, he went inside. Two steps down, he felt a rug under his feet. Carefully and slowly he walked all the way around the edge of the room, looking at everything in the dark.

"I wish I had a light," he thought. Then he began to look for matches. Finally he found some on a small table near one of the side windows. Cupping his hands carefully, Pete lit a match and got a quick look at the entire

77

room. It seemed to be like any room in a summer cottage.

"Nothing very special here," Pete thought, feeling disappointed. "Well, what did you expect?" he asked himself. "Crates of rifles sitting right in the middle of the floor?"

He thought of the pilot house. "Too small for crates," he told himself. He moved to the middle of the room.

"For a house boat that looks pretty fancy on the outside, this thing sure is awfully bare inside," Pete told himself. Then he thought of a reason.

Fannin probably figured he would not be here long. As soon as the rifles were taken out to the PT boat, he would leave. Pete was sure he knew how it would happen. First Fannin would tell a few people that business was bad. Then he would announce that he was looking for a new location. Then one morning he would be gone—and no one would ever see him again.

Suddenly Pete became alert. Was that the sound of Fannin's boat coming back? He was not sure, but he knew he had to hurry. He could see the moonlight shining on the water outside. Something was here, he knew it. The answer to all his questions—but he could not figure out what it was. He could almost *feel* it, but still the secret escaped him.

Once more Pete lit a match—and still he saw nothing. Then he went around the room, lighting matches every few feet. He looked closely at every piece of furniture. Nothing.

"Take it easy," he told himself, listening for the sound of Fannin's boat. He heard nothing—just silence and the ordinary sound of the water. It was a sound he had heard all his life, tiny waves against the side of a boat.

"Wait a minute!" he thought. The sound—something was wrong with it. But what? Why did it sound different? His mind whirled as he reached wildly for an answer. Then, like a wave knocking him down in the water, he knew.

The sound of the water was *inside* the boat!

Pete spun around, listening. The slap-slap-slap of the water was louder inside the room than it was from the outside. But that was crazy! There was no water inside the house boat, unless . . .

Then he heard the speed boat coming back.

He had to risk a few more seconds. He jumped to the edge of the rug, reached down and grabbed a corner. With a tug, he threw it back.

Now the sound of Fannin's boat was louder. Pete realized it was through North Inlet and back in the harbor. But there it was, the secret he had been looking for.

There was a hatch in the floor, about four feet square! What did it hide? A false bottom, where the rifles were hidden?

Pete could not wait to find out. The roar of the speed boat was close now.

Throwing the rug back in place, hoping it fell flat in the dark, Pete ran out to the deck.

The speed boat was less than a hundred yards away.

Keeping the cabin of the house boat between himself and the boat, Pete backed toward the rail. When he touched it, he ducked, slipped under the rail and let himself down into the water.

The speed boat reached the other end of the dock, and the engine was cut off. As Pete paddled quietly backwards through the water, he saw the big form of Bucko. Then Fannin's voice came across the water.

"Tie her up, Bucko. I am going inside."

Fannin walked down the dock toward Pete, stopped and looked out across the harbor. Pete forced himself to keep swimming quietly until he felt the marsh grass brush against his neck. In a moment he was safely hidden.

Moving carefully, Pete waded in to shore, walked far back into the pine woods and made a wide circle around the factory. He began running, both to keep warm and because he could not wait to tell Professor Nevins the news. When he reached the camp, a big fire was burning on the beach in front of the tent. The Professor was sitting on the sand smoking his pipe. Pete ran up to him.

"Well, I finally got the proof we were looking for," he said.

The Professor interrupted him. "First, get out of those swim trunks. You are shaking like a leaf."

Pete dried himself and began to tell his story. When he explained that he had gone aboard the house boat, the Professor shook his head.

"You shouldn't have done that, Pete."

"But I had to. Otherwise, I would never have found out what I did."

"Before you tell me," Professor Nevins interrupted, "did you ever think that when they got back to the house boat and put on the lights they would know someone had been there?"

"But *how?*" Pete asked.

"By the wet prints of your feet on the deck and floor of the cabin."

Pete felt a sudden, sick thud inside him.

CHAPTER SEVEN

Stay Off That Boat!

Pete and Professor Nevins woke early and settled down on the sand to hold a council of war.

"All right," Pete admitted. "I made a mistake last night. The question is, what do we do about it?"

"If Fannin and Bucko did see your foot prints," the Professor answered, "they must assume you found the hatch under the rug and know how they hide the rifles. That means they will move fast from now on—to finish their job and get away."

"I have to leave for home today," Pete said. "I promised Nick and my father."

"Get Nick to drive you to the hospital. See your father and tell him the whole story. Meantime, I can keep watch on the house boat. We should let your father decide."

Pete nodded and stood up. "I had better get started," he said.

A half hour later, Pete's tent and gear were in the boat and he was sailing back toward the Dana Boat Yard. It was a calm day, with only a faint breeze and hardly a ripple on the water.

Nick was not around when Pete got to the yard. He tied up his sailboat and carried his things to the office. Just as he came outside again, Nick drove up.

They sat on the back steps facing the yard while Pete told him the events of the night before. When he had finished, Nick said, "I guess we had better drive right back to town so you can see your father."

A few minutes later they walked up the steps of the hospital and went directly to Wesley Dana's room. When they reached the door, Nick stopped.

"Pete," he said, "I have to run over to Fish Town and check out a diesel engine. You go ahead and talk to your father alone."

Pete found Wesley Dana sitting up in bed, reading the newspaper. Mr. Dana looked up and, seeing Pete, smiled.

"Hello, Pete. Come in. Sit down—over here by the window."

Pulling the chair closer to the bed, Pete asked, "How are you feeling today, Dad?"

"Lots better," Wesley Dana said. "What brought you here so early? I didn't expect to see you until tonight."

"I had to come over here right away to see you . . . . I have something important to tell you about Fannin and the house boat."

"All right, Pete. What's on your mind?"

Pete related the whole story. He finished by saying, "I know I had no right to go aboard, but if I hadn't, I would never have found the answer."

"The point is, Pete, you had no right to go on Fannin's property without permission and without the law on your side."

Pete looked down at his hands for several seconds before speaking.

"I realize that, Dad."

Wesley Dana smiled. "I don't want you to think that I am being too hard on you. At your age I might have done the same thing."

"Are you going to call the Chief?" Pete asked.

"No, Pete."

"But why not, Dad?"

"What did you actually see, Pete? Did you see any rifles? No."

"Then we will never get Fannin," Pete said.

"Who said it is up to you to *get* him, Pete?"

A silence fell between them. Pete stood up.

"I guess I had better go. The Professor is waiting for me."

"I thought you were going to be working in the yard."

"I am, but Professor Nevins is waiting back on the

Dunes. I will be at work in the yard tomorrow, Dad. Nick said it was all right until then."

"You made one mistake going aboard the house boat, son," Mr. Dana said then. "Don't make it again. *Stay off that boat!*"

"Yes, sir, I will."

Pete went to the door. Half way through it he was stopped by his father's voice.

"Don't get me wrong, Pete. If Fannin *is* involved with guns, as you believe, I want to stop him, too. At the same time, I won't have you risk your neck to get the evidence. It is not your job. Remember that!"

When Pete's sailboat slid on to the beach in front of the Professor's camp, Professor Nevins was standing there to meet him. He looked angry.

"Pete," he said, "*every one of my nests has been broken up and scattered!*"

"What are you going to do?" Pete asked.

"Whether it is Fannin or not, I still have my work here. For five years I have done everything I could to help bird life. Now, in a few days, Fannin or someone has tried to wreck everything. I have decided to move my tent down to your old location. If I get away from North Inlet, perhaps the birds' nests will be left alone. I can still save my project here."

"But you are letting Fannin drive you off. I hate to see him win that way."

"Pete, I know how you feel, but the best way to save my project is to get away from here. Tell me, what did your father say?"

Pete shook his head. "My father says the hatch by itself is not evidence. I guess we have to *see* the rifles in there. But he told me not to go on the house boat again."

"I don't believe there is a secret hiding place under that floor at all," the Professor said. "I believe it is just a hole. My bet is that they have the crates of rifles lying right on the sandy bottom!"

"Of course!" Pete cried. "*That* is why Fannin wanted both ends of the house boat pulled in to the dock during the storm. He was afraid that we would be able to see the crates on the bottom in the morning!" Then he thought of something else. "But won't the rifles rust?"

"I remember the way they packed rifles in the army," the Professor said. "They put them in heavy grease and wrapped them tightly in tar paper. Water wouldn't hurt them. Even if there was rust, the guns could be cleaned as soon as they were taken out to the PT boat."

"That gives me an idea," Pete said, slowly. "Let's let them see us moving your camp down the beach near mine. Tonight we can build a big fire right out in the open, so they can see us from the house boat. We can sit around it for a couple of hours. Then, while you keep piling wood on the fire, I will go over to the house boat with the skin diving gear."

"They will see that only one of us is sitting by the fire!"

86

"No," Pete suggested, "not if we can make a dummy out of some of your clothes. Before I sneak away, I will seat the dummy by the fire. I will make a quick trip to find out just one thing—whether or not the crates are there under the house boat, on the bottom. I can take the lung for safety's sake. Then, if Fannin and Bucko come out, I can get away under water."

For the rest of the afternoon they were busy moving the Professor and setting up his tent a few yards away from Pete's old camping spot.

After that, Pete spent over an hour gathering a huge pile of wood for the fire. He had to go a long way down the beach in each direction to get enough, but finally the preparations were complete.

By the time the sun was beginning to settle in the western sky, they were cooking supper. Suddenly, a speed boat engine roared into life at the factory.

"So early?" Pete cried, jumping to his feet. "I wasn't sure they would take a chance and go out to the PT boat two nights in a row."

"Neither was I." The Professor was on his feet, too, peering into the darkness.

The boat roared away from the dock and headed out into the harbor.

"Sit down!" Pete said. "They are coming this way!"

A moment later the red speed boat shot past. It circled away and out into the harbor, then turned back toward the factory.

87

"*If we are right*, both Fannin and Bucko are beginning to get up crates from the bottom right now—to load them into the speed boat," Professor Nevins said.

"*If we are right*, the motor will start in about ten minutes," Pete said.

The Professor looked at his watch.

Pete was wrong—but only by three minutes. Exactly thirteen minutes later the speed boat motor burst into life again.

"That's it!" Pete said. "Time to go."

He got into the skin diving gear quickly, outside the circle of fire light. When he waded in, the water felt warm in contrast to the cool air of evening. He began swimming toward the house boat, making a wide circle to approach the dock from the far end.

Fifteen minutes later he had reached the boat and was hanging to the lowest step of the ladder, listening. The speed boat had long since passed through North Inlet and into the ocean.

"This is it," he thought.

He checked his face mask, closed his teeth on the mouth piece and turned on the air. He ducked under to check and found it working. Then he came up to listen for another moment.

All was quiet and he was ready. He went under.

Kicking with his feet and keeping his hands over his head to keep touch with the bottom of the house boat, Pete moved ahead step by step. There was no light at all

in the water, but he was sure he could find what he was after—if it was there.

A moment later his knee hit against something hard. He put his hand down and felt the corner of a box. With both hands, he traced the shape of it. When he took another step, his foot hit something else. It was another box! He let out a cry of excitement, got his mouth full of water and nearly choked. "Take it easy," he said to himself. "This is what you have been looking for. Find out how many are here and then get out—quick!"

A moment later he had the answer. Five crates.

Pete turned. "Come up slowly," he warned himself. He

was sure Fannin and Bucko had not returned. He knew that sound travels a long distance under water. He would have heard the speed boat motor.

His head broke the surface and he carefully pulled off his face mask. Breathing easily, he shook the water from his ears and listened. Still no sound of the speed boat. "Play it smart," he told himself. "Don't take chances. Move out right away."

He wanted to hurry back to tell the good news to the Professor. This was what they had been waiting for.

Pete pushed aside the marsh grass and began swimming out into the harbor. "These clouds will hide me if they do come back soon," he told himself.

He swam silently for the next few minutes. When he was half way back, he stopped to listen. From far away came the faint roar of a speed boat. Pete began to swim faster. Heavy dark clouds were passing in front of the moon, but there were still some clear spots in the sky.

"If the moonlight shines on me when the boat is anywhere near," he thought, "they can catch me."

He began to swim harder. In another ten minutes he would be back at the Dunes. A moment later the speeding boat burst through North Inlet and shot on to the calm surface of the harbor. At the same moment, the moon broke out of the clouds. Pete raised his head and saw the boat. It was coming straight at him!

For a second Pete was too surprised to do anything. Then he ducked beneath the surface of the water.

"Did they see me?" he wondered as the black water covered him. Before he could guess an answer, a roar filled his ears. Bubbles flashed against his face. He felt as if a ton of loose cotton had fallen on him. Fear came over him for an instant. "They passed right over me," he said to himself.

"It could have been an accident," Pete told himself, "or it could have been on purpose." It all depended on whether or not Fannin and Bucko had seen him. He had been caught in the moonlight for a moment. Perhaps the man at the wheel had seen the dark shape of his head in the water.

Quickly, he paddled upward. He felt the breeze strike his face. The moon was still out. He did not see the boat, but heard the engine behind him. He spun around in the water—just in time to see the boat make a wide circle.

Once more it headed directly toward him!

It had been no accident the first time. They had seen him all right, and had tried to run him down. Now they would try again. It was Pete, one eighteen-year-old boy, alone in the water against two men in a speed boat.

Where could he hide? "Of course!" Pete thought. "The best place of all—under water." For a moment, he had forgotten his face mask and his lung. Quickly he checked his mask, put in his mouth piece, turned on the air and sank beneath the water.

The feeling of roaring bubbles exploding down on his head was not as bad this time. He was ready for it. But

he knew what caused those bubbles—the blades of the speed boat's propeller, spinning at 3,000 RPMS.

"If that prop ever hits me," he thought, "good-by Pete Dana."

He saw it all now. Luck had handed Fannin a perfect chance to get him out of the way for good. He could take his time—all night if he had to. And when they found Pete's body next day, or next week, it would be an unfortunate boating accident.

The police might not even connect Fannin with it, at first. If the Professor said that Pete had been out in the harbor—and so had the speed boat—Fannin had only to say, "I couldn't see him in the dark. It's a terrible thing."

Now the boat was speeding in tight circles right over his head. "How do they know where I am? Pete wondered. "They can't see me." Then the answer came to him. "My air bubbles! Every time I breathe out, I am pointing a sign at myself. The moon must be out again. Well, there is no help for that. I can't stop breathing." This thought only led him to a new problem.

"I wonder how long these air tanks last?" he asked himself. "And I wonder how much of this tank we used up that day I had my first lesson?"

One thing became immediately clear to Pete. He could not waste time on the bottom of the harbor waiting for Fannin to leave. He had to try to save himself—and right now! If his air ran out, he would have to surface again, where he would be at Fannin's mercy.

"What is the best way?" Pete asked himself. Just then the speed boat passed over his head again. "I am almost in the middle of the harbor. The Town Dock is too far away, so I have three choices—the Dunes, the boat yard, or the house boat."

With almost no delay, he had his answer. "I will go over to the house boat," he thought. "They will never expect me to go that way." Suddenly, he reached down and felt his belt. He almost shouted when he found that the wrist compass was there. He had strapped one to each of the belts after his first lesson. Lifting it up close to his eyes, he found he could just read the face.

"Now I know I can find my way," he thought, "but when I get near shore, they will be able to see me in the shallow water." Then he thought of an answer to that, too. "A false trail," he decided. He thought out his plan and nodded to himself.

Pete dove a little deeper, lifted the compass to his eyes, and began swimming due west—toward the house boat. After about a minute, he turned north. Now he was swimming toward the Dunes. Twice during these few minutes the boat skimmed over his head.

Pete tried to swim very steadily, keeping in mind a picture of the harbor. He knew every tree and rock along the shore and in his head he had a map of every curve in the beach. Now his memory of exact distances was the only thing that could save his life.

It was a strange duel in the darkness. Neither person

could see his enemy, but each knew where the other was. If they touched in the dark—even once—only Fannin could win.

The boat passed over his head once more, this time quite close. Pete looked up and saw the glow of moonlight on the water. Without realizing it, he had let himself get too close to the surface.

"Fannin is right up there," he told himself. "He must see that the bubbles are heading for the Dunes."

He knew he was about eighty to one hundred yards from the house boat, which was off to his left. Up ahead, the Dunes were still over two hundred yards away. He looked up. The moonlight on the surface faded. Pete knew a cloud had passed over the moon.

"Now!" he said to himself.

Quickly he went to the bottom and swung the air tank off his shoulders. He put it on the sand but kept the mouth piece in his mouth. He opened the air tube wide and took several big breaths. Then he took off the belt and dropped it. He kept the mask on.

Turning off the air tube Pete took out the mouth piece, checked his direction on the compass and pushed off toward shore. If his judgment was right—and he could hold his breath that long—he could make it all the way to shore. He would end up in the marsh grass near the house boat . . . and there would be no bubbles to show Fannin which way he had gone!

Pete swam strongly the first half minute. He knew he

had stayed under for over a minute many times before. But now he was tired—and scared. As he pulled strongly with his arms and kicked with all his might, he kept hoping to feel marsh grass against his face.

His lungs seemed on fire—and still no marsh. "I can't make it," he thought. "Hang on," he told himself. "Ten more strokes. You can do it." He began to count to himself . . . "One . . . two . . . three . . . I can't go any . . . six . . . seven . . . eight . . ." Was that the boat over him? "Ten!"

He pushed upward and burst through the surface. He was almost to the marsh—only five yards away, Fannin's boat was still making circles far up the shore.

Pete waded quietly into the marsh, smiling to himself. "I beat him," he said, half aloud. "He had everything on his side, and still I beat him. All right, Mister Fannin, now it's my turn . . ."

When another cloud covered the moon, he stepped on to the shore.

CHAPTER EIGHT

We Are Pushing Our Luck

When Pete ran into the flickering light of the camp fire, Professor Nevins jumped to his feet.

"Pete! What happened? Are you all right? Where is the tank?"

Pete was panting from his run. He picked up a blanket lying on the ground. Wrapping himself in it, he moved closer to the fire and began to talk.

"But running you down would have brought the police to the factory by the dozens!" Professor Nevins broke in.

Pete shook his head. "It would have been just a boat accident!"

They both turned around as the sound of a speed boat motor shattered the night air again.

Pete jumped up from the fire and ran to the edge of

the water. He looked up and down the beach and out across the harbor. Then he walked back.

"What time is it?" he asked Professor Nevins. The Professor held his watch up to the fire light.

"Eleven-thirty," he said.

"They can't load all those rifles tonight! The tide is going out fast right now. They will be lucky to get back into the harbor from one more trip. They won't have high water again until morning."

"So, tomorrow may be their last night," the Professor added.

"Don't we have to be sure what their time table is?" Pete asked. "If we knew for sure they were pulling out, we could tell Dad."

"The first thing we do in the morning when it is light enough to see is to recover the tank," Professor Nevins replied. "Right now, how about some sleep?"

Pete grinned and shook his head. "I am too keyed up," he said as he followed the Professor into the tent.

Pete was wrong. He was asleep before the Professor had snapped off the lamp.

Getting the tank back from the harbor bottom was not as hard as Pete had expected. By luck, his second dive sent him directly to it. In the early morning mist not even the outlines of the house boat could be seen. Pete felt free to surface and swim back to shore with the tank strapped over one shoulder.

"Now to see if Nick can do without me one last day,"

Pete said. "All right if I borrow your boat, Professor?"

The Professor nodded. "Breakfast will be ready, if you can come back."

Pete shoved off in the Professor's small boat, set the starter cord, opened the choke, and pulled. The motor coughed, backfired, coughed again and caught. Pete threw it into gear and headed directly for the boat yard.

"Nick!" he called, rocking to a gentle landing by the dock. "Nick!"

He waited until Nick came around the corner, then stood up.

"Any chance you can give me one more day? Believe me, it's important, even though it sounds as if I'm trying to get out of working. Can you manage?"

Nick shook his head. "Lucky for you I finished that big paint job. I just put her in the water. But today is your last, no matter what."

"Thanks, Nick. I will do the same for you some day."

"What now?" Professor Nevins asked when Pete had returned, beached the boat and come up to the tent.

"Well, let's see. We need a safe place to start from, some spot on the ocean side where they won't be able to see us from the PT boat."

"PT boat? What are you talking about?"

Pete looked over at the Professor and smiled.

"Just thought of it. The perfect place! Over on the ocean side beyond North Inlet there is a small bay. Most people don't even know its name. We can come right

99

down through the woods to the edge of the water. There are big rocks there. I can get into my skin diving gear, slip into the water and go under. No one on watch out there on the PT boat would see me at all."

"What crazy plan are you talking about?" the Professor asked again.

"Not crazy, honestly," Pete replied. "Remember, we said that if we knew for sure what their time table was, Dad would have to move in a hurry. If I can get to the PT boat, I may find out exactly what the plans are. If not, we are no worse off than we are now."

"I'm not sure it makes very good sense, Pete."

"Listen, Professor Nevins, you and I are the only two people in Hidden Harbor who *know* the truth about Fannin. We have to do everything we can to stop him. Let me try this one last thing."

"I think you have talked me into too much already," Nevins replied. "I feel more like a spy than a teacher."

"This will be the very last thing, I promise."

Pete went into action fast, afraid the Professor would change his mind. They gathered the skin diving gear and began to move toward North Inlet, keeping behind the sand hills so that they could not be seen. Soon they were in the woods itself, completely protected from observation.

A few minutes later they were at the ocean beach. Pete stripped down to bathing trunks and got into the skin diving gear. Then, using the large rocks lying in the water near shore as cover, he moved into the water. Pete looked at his compass to get a line on the PT boat bobbing at anchor about 300 yards away.

"She is almost exactly northeast from here," he announced to the Professor.

"Can you swim a straight line to her?"

Pete nodded and walked out into the deeper water. He felt clumsy with the swim fins on until he began swimming, and then he felt the powerful thrust they gave him each time he kicked.

At fifteen feet below the surface, Pete had just enough light to read the compass by. He noticed that the ocean was much colder than the harbor had been the night before. He began to look upward and ahead, expecting at any moment to see the dark hull of the PT boat lying in the water.

"Could I have missed it?" he asked himself. He had no way to measure his progress under water and he could not be sure. Once again he looked at his compass. Everything seemed to be all right. He was exactly on course.

"Where is it?" Pete wondered.

Then he saw it, a dim shadow up ahead. A moment later, Pete began to swim toward the surface.

His head broke the water's surface exactly at the bow of the PT boat. It was rougher out here, so Pete knew he ran less risk of discovery. He took out his mouth piece.

"They were all in the stern the other day," Pete thought.

He dived and when he came up again, he found a good hand hold on the rudder, just under the surface.

Pete heard the clear bang of a door being slammed on deck, then the sound of two voices. The PT boat rose and fell in the small waves with a slapping sound that made it difficult for Pete to hear the conversation on deck. For the next few minutes he heard only a few words—never a whole sentence.

Suddenly Pete heard, ". . . wish we could get away from here . . ."

"Me, too . . . like to know what is taking so long."

". . . more rifles . . . we are pushing our luck." The two men went on talking.

" . . . told me that tonight was the last . . ."

"Are you sure?" the second man asked.

Whatever the first one answered was lost to Pete as

the PT boat slapped up and down, sending flying spray into his face. Pete decided he had heard enough. "I had better get back and tell Professor Nevins," he thought.

The return trip was easy. Pete was back in the shelter of the rocks along shore in five minutes. As he slipped off his mask and turned off the air, Pete spoke to the Professor.

"There is no doubt about it. They have the rifles on board and Fannin is going to make the final delivery tonight."

"Is that what you heard?" the Professor asked, a note of excitement in his voice that he could not hide.

"Absolutely!"

The Professor took Pete's hand and helped pull him up behind the rocks.

"What next?" Pete wondered out loud.

"Get to the hospital as fast as we can, and you tell your father everything."

"If *you* tell him what we just heard out there, he will really have to believe us," Pete broke in.

"*Me!* Why me?"

"Because I did everything wrong on that first search. He believes I act first and think afterward. But he knows you don't. He will listen to you."

The Professor looked thoughtful. "You mean, I go to the hospital while you stay here?"

"Isn't that the best way to be sure we know what is happening?" Pete argued. "If we both go into town,

Fannin may leave on the PT boat and we wouldn't even know it."

"What will you do while I'm gone?" Nevins asked.

"Stay here and keep an eye on the PT boat."

"Stay *where?*"

"Here—in the water back of these rocks."

The Professor nodded, but he was still thinking. "All right, but on one condition—that you don't go near the boat."

"But suppose I *have* to go out there for some reason?"

"No!"

"But we can't tell what might happen while you are gone! Suppose the only way I can keep track of them is to follow the boat?"

The Professor sighed. "Pete, I am trying to get it into your head that your part of this is *finished.* If they head out to sea you just have to let them go. If the police want to get the Coast Guard, that is up to them. But it is *not* your job to stop them—or to go anywhere near them. You told me what Fannin tried to do to you last night. Well, you can be sure those men out there would do the same thing if you got in their way."

Now Pete was silent.

"Well, Pete, what about it?" Professor Nevins asked.

Pete looked over at Professor Nevins and smiled.

"You win."

"You won't go near the PT boat?"

"No."

"All right, and keep your promise this time! I'm on my way into town."

From the cover of the trees, Professor Nevins turned and waved once to Pete. Then he was gone. Pete was alone in the water.

CHAPTER NINE

Shark Bait

When the Professor was out of sight, Pete turned back toward the PT boat. As it swung around at anchor, Pete saw the two men sitting in the stern. No one else was on deck.

Suddenly the door of the wheel house on the PT boat opened, and a third man came out.

"What's going on now?" Pete asked himself. Pete watched with growing interest as they began to coil lines and hang them on hooks on the side of the wheel house.

As he watched, and the men continued to clear the decks, Pete felt both excitement and anger growing in him. He knew the Professor could not be even half way to the Town Dock by now, and here the PT boat might be leaving.

"This is just what I was talking about," he said to himself. "I was afraid something like this might happen!"

Now the three men returned to the bow and gathered around something that Pete could not see. Whatever it was, it was hidden by the high rail that had been built up around the bow. As Pete watched, a clanging sound came across the water.

For a moment Pete did not know what it was. But then he realized in a rush.

"They are pulling up anchor!" he almost shouted. He looked around wildly, hoping to see someone near who could help him.

"You dope," he said to himself, "even if there were someone, what could you do?"

If the PT boat was going to be stopped, Pete would have to do it—alone. But how? "If he were on board," he thought, "it would be easy." But he was not and there was no way for him to get on board.

As he was thinking these things, the clanging noise stopped. While Pete watched, the men walked back to the stern and sat down on the deck again.

Pete smiled to himself, feeling foolish.

"I know what it is," he thought to himself, "they were just getting *ready* to leave. They pulled up the anchor chain part way so they can get away quicker tonight. But they won't go until they get that last load of rifles from Fannin."

Pete felt his heart beating fast. "We should have

brought a two-way radio," he thought. "Then, if the boat started to leave, I could have let the Professor know." There had been no time for such careful planning. "All right," he told himself, "I will have to get along by myself!"

Pete made a decision.

"If I moved closer to the PT boat, I might learn for sure what they were planning. If I thought they were about to take off, I could get back to the Professor's camp and sail back to town."

Pete looked around and saw the one place where he could get closer. About half way between the beach and the PT boat was a large rock, reaching up out of the water.

"Too bad it's right in line with North Inlet," Pete thought, "but Fannin and Bucko won't come out here yet. It would be too dangerous."

He slipped his mask on, turned on the air supply from his tank, and dived under the surface.

Pete made the trip under water using the wrist compass. He came up exactly next to the rock, on the side away from the boat.

"This is a lot better," he thought. "I can see them much more clearly. Why, the way the wind is blowing in toward shore, I may even be able to hear something they say once in a while."

For the next few minutes, Pete kept his eyes fixed on the boat. Nothing happened. His back was turned toward

North Inlet and the beach and anything that might be happening in the harbor.

Pete wondered whether the Professor had reached the hospital. He was getting tired, holding on to the rock. The breeze which had come up made the water rough. He could hear nothing but the splashing of small waves breaking on the rock right next to his head.

Then it happened. Nothing had warned Pete. A heavy arm hooked around his throat and slammed the back of his head against something hard.

He started to shout with surprise. But his words were cut off as the beefy arm pulled him in tighter.

Out of the corner of his eye, Pete caught a flash of red paint. He realized someone had come up behind him in a boat, and red paint meant only one thing to him— Fannin's boat.

Pete grabbed the wrist of the heavy arm and tried to pull it away from his neck, but he could not move it. He knew only too well who had that much strength—Bucko.

Still not a word had been said. Not a sound had been made.

Then Pete felt himself being lifted. In one motion, he was out of the water and over the side into the boat. Before Pete had time to do more than catch a look at Fannin's face, he found himself thrown down on to the boat bottom. His mask was knocked off and a big foot was planted in the middle of his back to hold him down.

He struggled for breath.

"Shut up, kid, and don't move," Bucko said in his deep voice. Then Fannin spoke.

"The idea, boy, is to stop you from meddling in our business—once and for all."

It was clear that Fannin felt sure Pete had found out about the guns. Pete had to bluff, if he could. It was the only thing he could do right now to save himself.

"What are you talking about?" he gasped. "Here I am, skin diving, and you guys come out in the water and grab me. What have I done?"

Fannin laughed softly.

"It's what you aren't going to do that is important."

Bucko started to row toward the PT boat, while Fannin kept his foot in the middle of Pete's back. Lying on the wet bottom of the boat, Pete decided to remain quiet.

"The worst part of all this," Pete thought, "is that Professor Nevins is probably just about reaching the Town Dock by now. After he has explained everything, they still have to get the police boat and come all the way around here to the PT boat . . . provided the PT stays put."

He was calmer now, but it did not make him feel any better to know that Fannin thought he was dangerous enough to kidnap in broad daylight.

"The next question," he told himself, "is what are they going to do with me?"

Bucko rowed strongly and then Pete heard a voice shout from somewhere over his head.

"All right, boys, here we are! Grab this line!" It was Fannin, shouting to the men on the PT boat.

"And we got something else for you to grab, too," Bucko added.

Pete felt Bucko pull roughly at the canvas straps of the air tank on his shoulders. Then Bucko raised him up to the edge of the PT boat deck. There, three pairs of hands grabbed him.

"Get him down below and out of sight," Fannin ordered. "And make sure he can't get out. I don't want him in the way tonight. One more trip and you boys will be gone. By morning, you will be miles out to sea. Even the Coast Guard won't be able to stop you."

"And what do we do with *him?*" one of the men asked Fannin, pointing at Pete.

Bucko laughed loudly. "He looks like shark bait to me."

"I will make up my mind what to do with him later," Fannin answered. "So far as I know, no one but this kid has made any connection between the house boat and the PT boat."

"That's what *you* think!" Pete said in an angry voice. The moment he spoke he regretted it.

Fannin turned to him, and spoke in a cold voice.

"Oh? Probably your bird-watching friend. Well, if anyone comes around looking for you, I think *you* will be the one to regret it."

This time Pete kept quiet. He had already said too much. But at least he had not told them the Professor was on his way to get the police.

Two of the men lifted him to his feet and shoved him through a door just behind the wheel house.

"Get down there, and don't try anything," one of them said roughly.

Pete found himself at the head of a small iron ladder. Four steps led down to the engine room. When he got to the bottom, Pete looked around quickly. Two huge diesel engines occupied most of the space in the center. Along each side were three very large fuel tanks. It was clear to Pete that this PT boat had been fitted out at great expense so she could remain at sea for long periods of time.

"Bring him over here," the first man said.

Pete was pulled toward the rear of the room. One of the men began tying Pete's hands behind his back while the other bound his feet. Pete tried to keep his arms stiff as he was tied. A minute later, when the man finished and Pete let his arms go loose, he could feel that the rope was not completely tight.

The first man shoved him down on the deck.

"Stay there," he said, "and don't make any trouble."

Pete said nothing as the men turned and climbed up the ladder to the deck.

Alone in the dark engine room, Pete tried once again to figure out where Professor Nevins would be at that moment.

"By now the Professor and the police ought to be heading down to the Town Dock to get the police boat," Pete told himself. "In another hour, at most, they should have me out of here."

Pete jumped with surprise when the engines started with a roar. He felt his heart beating faster as first one and then the other engine was raced to a full roar. The PT was getting under way! But as the engines shut off again he felt better.

"They aren't going any place," he said to himself, "not yet, at any rate."

After five more minutes or so, the engines were turned on and off again, one at a time. Pete realized that the men were only testing them for tonight.

"That makes sense. Once they leave here, they don't want anything to go wrong." Now the waiting became twice as hard to bear. Pete's wrists and hands were getting cold from the ropes around them—although they were not really tight.

"Holy smoke, I can't hold out here forever," he thought. "How long do they expect me to wait?"

Another fifteen minutes dragged by. "Something must have gone wrong," Pete decided. "It's up to me . . . I guess."

Twisting his hands furiously, he tried to free himself from the ropes. He could almost slip his hands out, but not quite. If he could only get one loop of the rope off, he realized, the rest might be easy.

He looked around. A few feet away, a bolt was sticking out of a wooden brace that held one of the fuel tanks in place. Rolling over, Pete slid up to it backwards until he could touch it with his hands. Working carefully, he hooked one loop of the rope over the end of the bolt, trying to pull it off his hands. Each time he caught the bolt and pulled against it the loop only slid off it.

Suddenly, he felt a loop slip from his hands. In another second he was free. He untied the rope around his feet and stood for a moment. Then he moved quietly to the foot of the iron ladder. He listened for a few seconds, heard nothing, and started climbing.

At the top, Pete found the knob on the door that led out on deck. He twisted the knob, pushed the door open and plunged out on to the deck. All he could think of was a short dash to the rail, a dive over the side . . . and the safety of the sea.

He had taken only two steps when a strong arm went around him.

"Well, well," a rough voice said, "the little bird wanted to fly away."

It was the man who had tied him. Pete rolled over on his back and looked up. The man was standing over him, blocking his path to the rail, and looking down at him in a frightening way.

"Now, you know you shouldn't have done that, little bird," the man said. "You heard Mr. Fannin's invitation. He asked you to stay with us—and you might hurt his feelings if you left us all of a sudden. He might think you didn't like us." The man did not laugh. In fact, Pete wondered as he looked at his face, if he had ever laughed.

"You did it again," Pete told himself. "You ran out without thinking—right into their arms."

Pete did not even try to fight, as the men lifted him to his feet and carried him through the engine room door.

This time the knots were tight—so tight he could feel his hands going to sleep. For half an hour Pete lay there, too miserable to do anything. Then his wrists began to ache so much he was forced to move. He propped himself up in a sitting position with his back against one of the fuel tanks. From where he sat, he was staring over the two diesel engines at the fuel tanks on the opposite side of the boat.

Pete became calmer. He thought, "At least I can do one thing. I can *think*."

It grew dark in the next hour. With the fading light, his hopes sank. Worst of all, he could not come up with a single idea. He felt as if his mind were frozen. It was easy to say *"Think,"* he discovered, but a lot harder to do it. How could he possibly get out? He was tied up and locked in. He had already made a wild run for it, but had only been caught and tied up more tightly. What did smart people do in a spot like this, he wondered?

Then he got the beginning of an idea.

"How would Nick think if he were here?" he asked himself. "And how would the Professor go about it?" He nodded to himself. This was better. "And my father—what would he do."

This seemed like a situation Nick might be able to handle best, if anyone could. When it came to boats, no one could top Nick. But there was something else. It came to Pete as if the Professor had spoken to him out of the dark. "Let the police handle Fannin. That is not your job." That is what the Professor had said. It was good advice then and it was still good.

"Then what I have to do," Pete thought, "is delay this boat long enough for the police to get here. Sooner or later, they will realize I have been gone too long and they will come after me. So I have to keep the boat here until then—*somehow.*"

Pete heard a new sound and knew right away what it was. A small boat had come alongside.

"It must be Fannin," Pete thought. "I have only a

few minutes while they bring the rifles aboard, then I will find out what is going to happen to me."

He was right. For the next five minutes he listened to the sound of bumping and scraping on deck. The door at the top of the ladder opened and a beam of light shot through the darkness and fell on Pete. He did not look at it, but kept his eyes on the fuel tank opposite him.

"Yes, he's still there," a rough voice said. "He hasn't moved this time."

Pete heard Fannin's voice say, "Well, keep him there. And don't get rid of him until you are well out to sea."

"Right," the other voice said.

"Get moving as soon as we leave," Fannin added sharply.

The door slammed, and Pete heard no more except the sound of steps hurrying back and forth on deck. Then the sound of a small boat bumping against the side of the PT boat told Pete that Fannin and Bucko were about to take off.

"Help must be on the way by now," Pete thought. "The only thing he could do would be to delay the PT boat and hope that the police would catch up to them. But how?"

He had been staring at the fuel tanks but he had not really been looking. Now he noticed something, and realized that he could stop the PT boat any time he wanted!

"Should I do it now?" Pete asked himself. "No! Better

wait until we have started. Let them start first, and then I will stop the boat."

He smiled to himself grimly in the darkness. "If anything will work, this will."

Pete jumped as the two big engines came to life. He heard the anchor chain being hauled in. When that noise stopped, he knew what was next.

With a heavy roar, the PT boat started out to sea. Pete could feel the boat swing in a wide circle as it headed for open water.

CHAPTER TEN

Stand By or We Fire

For several minutes the diesels ran at high speed, then someone in the pilot house cut the power and the engines settled down to a steady beat. Since the moment the PT boat had headed out to sea, Pete had been studying the fuel tanks on the other side of the engines.

Now he twisted around so he could look at the one directly behind him. He saw that just over his head was a fuel shut-off valve set right against the side wall of the tank. A piece of copper tube ran from this in a long curve to the forward end of the engine room where it was connected to the port engine.

"That's good enough," Pete told himself. "Knocking out one engine will do the trick."

The PT boat turned sharply, throwing Pete flat on the

engine room floor. A second later, the engines were in high again. He felt the boat rush ahead under the increased power.

"*Now* what is going on?" Pete wondered. "Maybe they saw something! It might be the regular Coast Guard patrol boat!"

Pete twisted around. He would have to stand up to reach the cut-off valve. Putting his back against the tank, he pushed with his feet against one side of the engine bed. By rocking his shoulders from side to side, he was able to slide his back up the side of the tank. It was slow but sure work. When he was almost on his feet, someone up in the wheel house cut the power again. The PT boat slowed suddenly, the bow dropped and the boat pitched sharply. With his hands tied, Pete could not save himself. Once more, he fell flat on the engine room deck.

Pete groaned aloud as he tried to turn over, and a sharp pain ran through his shoulder.

"No time to waste," he told himself. "Time is passing too fast already."

Again, Pete put his back against the tank and started to push himself up with his feet. This time he was in pain as he rocked his shoulders to move upward. Sweat broke out on his face.

Finally he was on his feet. With the PT boat going more slowly, he found the engine room floor was more nearly level. He lifted his tied hands as far as he could behind his back, reaching for the cut-off valve.

Straining, Pete stood on his toes and forced his hands upward. Finally he had touched the valve.

"Now, what?" he asked himself. With his hands bound with rope, what could he do?

The PT boat was moving steadily—moving farther and farther away from shore, Pete was certain. He knew they would be passing the entrance to Hidden Harbor in only a few minutes. Once past that, his chances of being saved would reach the vanishing point.

"Do it," he thought. "Don't worry how, just do it. What's the matter with you? You used to be a man of action."

He turned around and leaned over until his fingers could hook on to the valve handle. It was hard to hold firm with the PT boat rocking as it was. Finally, however, he twisted his entire body and felt the handle move.

"Hang on, boy," he thought. "You can do it!"

Once again he gripped and twisted. Again the handle moved. Turn by turn, Pete slowly moved the cut-off valve to the closed position. He dropped down in a sitting position.

It took only minutes for things to begin happening.

First the engine near him coughed, ran easily again for a few seconds, missed a beat . . . once . . . twice . . . and finally cut out altogether.

A moment later, the other engine was down to slow speed. Then someone on deck pressed the starter. There was a grinding sound for several seconds and then there was only silence. The starter turned again. Once more it groaned—and stopped. Again several seconds passed.

"Now!" he thought. "Open it!"

He began turning the valve handle open again. This time it was not as hard. He knew how to do it and it went faster.

Pete had just settled down once more on the engine room deck when the door at the head of the ladder opened and two men came down.

"Must be a fuel line," one of them said in the darkness.

"Terrible time for *that* to happen," the other answered.

A flash light snapped on and the two men came over to the port engine. The man with the flash light checked it over, tinkering with one part after another.

"Seems to be all right here," he said. "Let's have a look at the tank and line." He flashed the light briefly on Pete.

"Our friend here seems quiet enough," he said. Then he looked at the cut-off valve. "Nothing wrong here," he said. He ran his fingers along the entire length of the copper tube to the place where it was connected into the engine. "No break in the line," he said. "Go up and tell them to try again."

The other man left and in a few seconds Pete heard the familiar sound of the engine starter. After turning over a dozen times or so, the engine suddenly roared into deafening life.

The man with the flash light paid no more attention to Pete. After listening to the engine for a few moments he turned and started up the ladder. By the time the door slammed above, both engines were running at a steady, throbbing pace.

Pete immediately got to his feet. This time the entire process went much faster from beginning to end: Pete got the valve closed . . . the engine stopped . . . Pete scarcely got it open again before the men appeared. Now they were really angry.

"Don't ask *me*," the man with the flash light said as they came down the ladder. "I tell you, there was nothing wrong with that engine this morning. It was perfect."

"Then why did it stop?" the other man asked.

"I don't know, and shut up!" the first man answered hotly.

Once again he checked, then sent the other man up to the wheel house. Once again the engine started and the man with the light disappeared. This time he had not even looked at Pete.

Pete allowed a minute to pass.

"We must be just passing Main Inlet, or are already past it," he thought. "I can't waste any more time."

He was still closing the cut-off valve when the door opened and the flash light shone directly on him from the top of the ladder.

"So that's it!" a voice said. "I should have thought of that before. Our young friend is not so helpless after all!"

In the next minute, the two men had tied Pete flat on the deck to some pipes.

"Well, that's it," he thought. "I have done all I could. At least I made them lose time. And maybe somebody on shore has—"

His thought was cut off as he heard running steps on the deck over his head. Then he heard shouting. A moment later the engines were thrown into high speed.

Pete did not dare to hope, but his heart began to pound. The next moment the door at the top of the ladder was pulled open. The shouting on deck became louder and the running foot steps continued. One voice came through to Pete clearer than the rest.

"Get that kid up here on deck!"

Two men came tumbling down the ladder, cut Pete loose, roughly dragged him up the ladder, shoved him through the door and threw him flat on the deck. He was surprised to see how dark it was. He could not tell how long he had been below, but it must have been for hours.

Twisting his head around, he saw that there were two men with field glasses standing in the bow. They were staring out to sea. One shouted back to the wheel house.

"It's getting closer," he said, "but I still can't tell what it is."

"Is it cutting across our course?" the man in the wheel house shouted back.

There was a pause and then the man in the bow answered, "I think so."

"Where did it come from?" the man in the wheel house asked.

"Right out of Main Inlet—from the harbor."

"How big is it?"

The man in the bow raised his glasses again and looked off toward the north. "Not too big. Maybe thirty, thirty-five feet."

Pete felt a glow of excitement. That sounded like the police boat.

"Let's head out a little and see if it still follows us," the man in the wheel house said.

Pete felt the boat swing. He had thought that the PT boat would head south when it left Hidden Harbor. But before it could do that, it had to go directly east for fifteen miles to round the point of Cape Ann. "If that is the police boat," he thought, "it came just at the right time."

Then a thought struck him.

"That police boat can never catch this PT. She can make at least forty knots. The police boat never hit thirty in its best days."

There was only one thing that could catch this PT, Pete realized, and that was a Coast Guard cutter.

The man in the wheel house called out again.

"Are they still coming?"

The man in the bow called back, "Yes, but no closer. If that's their full speed, they will never catch us."

For the next five minutes—the longest Pete had ever

lived through—nothing more happened. Pete lay with his cheek pressed into the deck and his shoulder aching. What he would have given right that second to be standing on the gas float at the boat yard, looking out over the harbor! No trouble, no Fannin, no PT boat. Just a lovely peaceful summer evening in Hidden Harbor.

Worst of all was thinking about his father, and Nick, and the Professor. They were the very best people in the world. No boy ever had a better father than Wesley Dana, or better friends than Nick and Professor Nevins. How right they had been about not acting without thinking. No matter how smart Pete had been down in the engine room, he was in trouble because he had not stopped to think. If he had not moved out to that rock, if he had gone back to town with John Nevins . . . if he had ever listened to anyone . . .

"Forget it," he told himself. "It is too late to think about these things now." He rolled on to his back and stared up at the sky. That seemed a lot better than looking down at the deck only an inch from his nose.

Suddenly, the darkness above Pete's head was cut by a brilliant shaft of light. It came from the sea to the north. Pete lifted his head and looked toward the bow. He saw the figures of the two men standing there, caught in the strong light. Then one of them turned and looked toward the wheel house with a helpless expression on his ugly face.

"What's that?" the man shouted.

"I don't know," the voice in the wheel house answered.

"You have the glasses—look and see!"

"How can I see anything? I'm half blinded right now!" the man said in an angry voice.

"One of you go to the stern. Maybe you can see from there. Now, jump!"

One of the men ran toward the back of the boat.

As Pete looked at the side of the cabin over his head, the bright light moved slowly back. A few seconds later it moved forward again and fixed itself on the wheel house. The man who had gone to the back of the boat came pounding back to the wheel house, shouting as he ran.

"It is the Coast Guard. They are coming up on us fast!"

"Get rid of the kid!" the man in the wheel house ordered. "Throw him over the side!"

"What good is that? We don't even have time to get rid of the guns!"

"You heard me," shouted the man in the wheel house.

"But they might see him in the light!"

"Do what I tell you. They have that light right here on the wheel house. If you dump the kid over on the far side of the boat, they won't see him. At least we won't face a kidnaping rap."

The two men jumped for Pete. As they leaned over to take hold of him, Pete bent his knees back to his chest. With a strong kick, he sent one of the men flying. The man slammed against the rail head first and slid to the deck without making a sound. The second man jumped back.

"All right, kid," he said, "you asked for it."

He reached into his back pocket and brought out a long wrench. Moving in on Pete carefully, he held the wrench up. "I will just quiet you down first," he said.

"Did you get rid of the kid?" the man in the wheel house yelled.

"Not yet. He knocked Eddie out."

"Knocked him out! I thought he was tied!"

"He is, but he can still kick!" The man with the wrench moved in slowly, keeping his eyes on Pete's feet.

"One more minute," Pete thought. "Just one more minute and I may still make it." He had his feet pulled back again as the man stepped in closer and brought his arm down.

Pete kicked with all his might and rolled to the side.

At that instant, the PT boat made a sudden move as both engines were thrown into full speed. The man with the wrench lost his balance. He threw his hands out to protect himself and the wrench fell from his hand and slid across the deck in the dark.

Just then the man in the wheel house shouted. "Forget the kid. Come on up here, I need you."

"What are you going to do?"

"That cutter is heading us off. If I cut between Barton's Reef and the shore, they won't be able to stop us. By the time they go around, we will be out at sea."

A mental picture of this part of the coast flashed in Pete's mind. Some boats could cut in behind Barton's Reef he knew, without hitting bottom. And it was also true that the cutter could not do it. Pete knew that for a fact. But there was something else.

"What is it?" he asked himself. "It is something Nick told me once." He was tired and cold. He ached all over and he could not think straight. Then it came to him.

"I know!" he thought. "A boat this size can't go behind Barton's Reef except at full high tide. And that will not be for at least another hour! They are going to pile this boat up on the rocks!"

Tied up as he was, it was a not a very pleasant thought. Off in the distance a voice shouted.

"Stand by to be boarded!" The voice had authority.

That could only be one thing, Pete knew—the Coast Guard. But if the PT boat got to Barton's Reef first, the cutter would have to swing around the reef and out to sea before it could again give chase.

"You are heading for Barton's Reef," the voice called through the darkness. "Stand by to be boarded or we will fire on you!"

The man in the wheel house shouted, "Hold that kid up in the light. Then they won't fire on us."

By now the man called Eddie was sitting up on deck, shaking his head to clear it. As he got to his feet, the one who had tried to hit Pete with the wrench came out of the wheel house. Together, the two men picked Pete up and held him upright in the bright shaft of the cutter's search light. Pete closed his eyes.

The PT boat sped on. Pete waited for the sound of gun fire. It did not come. Pete realized he had been seen and recognized.

The voice called across the water again.

"You are heading toward Barton's Reef. If you try to go through, you will tear the bottom out of your boat. You can only use that channel at dead high water!"

"Don't listen," the man called Eddie said. "They are just saying that to make us stop. They know we can get away and they are trying to fool us."

"Don't worry," the man at the wheel said. "I am going through. It is our only chance now. Drop that kid and come up here. I need one of you to look at the chart and one to spot the rocks for me."

The two men dropped Pete and headed for the wheel house on the run. After that there were several seconds of silence. The cutter's light was on the PT boat but there was no further talk. Then Pete saw that the light was getting dimmer.

"They are slowing down," he thought. "That means we are close. The cutter is starting to move outside Barton's Reef."

When the PT boat hit, it came all of a sudden.

The bow lifted a little, then the sound of tearing wood reached Pete's ears. The boat tipped and shook along its entire length. Someone in the wheel house cut the power.

"Get down below and see how bad it is!" the man at the wheel shouted.

Someone ran out of the wheel house, dashed past Pete and disappeared through the engine room door. A moment later he ran back to the wheel house.

"Mike, she's going down!" he shouted. "Water is pouring in like a waterfall."

"All right, don't get excited," the man in the wheel house said. "The main thing is to try to get away. The cutter can't come in here. We still have a chance."

"What about the kid?" Eddie asked.

"He's tied up. Leave him where he is."

The other man spoke up. "Why don't you try to run her up on shore? The chart doesn't show any houses along here."

"Maybe you are right. Might as well take a chance. I hope the engines keep turning."

Lying on deck, Pete heard the two engines rumble to life.

"Now I have a chance," he thought. "If they run this thing up on shore, she will not sink completely. When they go over the side, maybe I can get up in the bow and keep out of the water."

He felt the boat swing around and start slowly toward shore. Pete remembered that Barton's Reef was about three hundred yards off the beach.

"I should hear the waves in just a little while," he thought.

A half minute passed as the engines turned over slowly. Then Pete heard the waves crashing on the shore.

"At this speed she is going to turn over!" he thought.

The next moment he felt the bow lift again as the boat entered the first line of swells rolling toward the beach. The PT began to twist to one side. Pete knew what was happening. His life depended on what the captain did in the next few seconds.

"Give her the gun!" he shouted. "Head her straight into the beach or she will turn over!"

The moments until he heard the engines thrown into full speed were terrible ones for Pete. When the next wave rose up under them, Pete knew that for the moment they were all right. First the stern lifted, then the bow went up as the wave rolled right under them.

As the next wave came up, Pete heard the sound of the roaring waves just ahead. With nothing to hold on to and no way to protect himself, he could only hope for the best.

"If we go over," he thought, "I won't have a chance."

CHAPTER ELEVEN

The Best Part

The PT boat roared into the middle of the breaking waves. A wave hit her stern and drove her ahead of it at express-train speed. Plunging, she was hit by a second wave. Her speed increased and she began to roll. Pete braced himself, waiting for the crunch of her bow on the sand.

The third wave broke over the stern, sending foam and tumbling water along the decks. It washed Pete forward along the deck, completely covering him.

At the same instant, the boat hit. The bow lifted high again, as it had when it struck the rocks of Barton's Reef. A loud scraping sound filled the air. Then the PT boat came down with a thump as the wave set her on the beach and washed back to sea. The next wave, slamming into her stern, drove her a few feet higher on the beach.

The three men came tumbling out of the wheel house.

Without a word or a glance at Pete they ran to the rail and leaped over the side. Pete heard each of them splash in the shallow water.

"I made it," Pete told himself. "I made it!"

Somehow, he knew that now he was going to be all right. And the very next thought that came into his head was that Fannin's men were getting away.

A beam of light much smaller than the one from the Coast Guard cutter shot across the bow of the PT boat. Pete sat up on deck and saw that it was shining on the men as they climbed up a high sand hill on the beach. A loud voice cut through the night air.

"Stop where you are. This is the police. Don't move or we will fire! Put your hands in the air!"

Pete pushed himself to his feet and looked out to sea. Just beyond the breaking waves, the police boat was moving along slowly, its search light fixed on the hill. He looked back to the men. They were standing in the glare of the search light, but they did not have their hands up. Suddenly they broke into a run and headed in toward land.

A burst of gun fire sounded over Pete's head. Little sprays of sand flew up just behind the running men who stopped suddenly and threw their hands in the air.

Pete saw four men from the police patrol leap into a small boat, and head toward shore. As he watched the skill with which the boat was handled, Pete was proud of Hidden Harbor. Only men born and brought up on

the edge of the sea could bring a small boat in through breaking waves like that without being swamped.

When the boat touched land, two men with guns in their hands leaped out and ran up the beach. One of the others hurried down toward the PT boat. As he got close, Pete saw who it was.

"Nick!" he shouted. "Nick! Over here!"

Nick's voice came back to him across the sand. "Are you all right?"

"Sure, but climb up here and untie me."

A moment later Pete was free and he and Nick had thrown their arms around each other as if they had not seen each other for years. Then Nick spoke.

"We have to get back to the police boat."

"What about them?" Pete asked, pointing to the men on the beach.

"They are being taken out to the state road. We used the boat ship-to-shore radio to call the sheriff. He will pick them up. We have to go back after Fannin!"

In his whole life there had never been anything for Pete like the next hour. First there was the wild ride through the waves until Pete, Nick and the police who had stayed with them reached the police boat safely. Then, as the boat swung around and headed for Hidden Harbor at full speed, there was another happy meeting —this time with Professor Nevins who was waiting on board.

"What happened? What took you so long?" Pete asked.

"Well," Professor Nevins told him, "after I tied up the boat at the Town Dock and went to the hospital, your father was gone! The doctor said he was feeling so well that he insisted on going home. So I drove out to your house, but he was not there, either!"

"Holy smoke! Where was he?"

"Nick had picked him up, so I had to drive all the way to Nick's house in Fish Town.

"As soon as I told your dad the story, he called the Chief. It seems the Chief was already getting a crew together. I will tell you why later. By the time the Chief had his men down at the Town Dock, another hour had passed," the Professor went on. "It was nearly dark by

137

then. We didn't know whether to look for you at North Inlet or head directly for the PT boat. We decided to pick you up first, to be sure."

"And you couldn't find me," Pete broke in.

"Right," Nick said, continuing the story. "But the worst part was that just as we got to the ocean, we saw the PT boat leaving. We looked all along the shore for you, but no luck."

"Did you think they had me on board?" Pete asked.

"We couldn't be sure, but we were afraid so," Nick answered.

Professor Nevins took up the story again. "We came back across the sand to the police boat and called by radio to the Coast Guard." He paused and looked straight at Pete. "Here is some news for you. The Coast Guard already knew all about the PT boat. A cutter had been standing by. District Headquarters was pretty sure what was going on. So was the Chief. He didn't tell your father he suspected Fannin because it was none of our business. He did not want you or me or anyone else meddling in the affair. He was having trouble enough without any of us getting in the way."

"That may have been why he was so annoyed at having to search the place," Pete added thoughtfully.

The Professor, who had paused for breath, now went on, "The Coast Guard was going to board the PT as soon as she tried to get away. The police were going to do the same thing with the house boat. The only thing is, none of them had figured that you would be aboard the PT boat."

"How could they?" Pete agreed.

"So when the Coast Guard recognized you in the search light, the only chance left was that the PT would wreck itself on Barton's Reef and not sink."

"And the police boat had to come looking for me instead of going to the house boat?"

Professor Nevins nodded. "All the plans got messed up."

"One thing has me puzzled," Nick said. "Why did the PT boat stop three times?"

Pete smiled. "I did that. I cut off the fuel to one engine and the crew kept rushing down to the engine room for repairs. But each time I got the fuel turned on again before they arrived, so they couldn't find out what was wrong."

Professor Nevins ran his hand over his hair and grinned at Pete. "That was using your head."

The police boat began to make a sharp turn and Pete stood up in the small cabin. Looking out a port hole, he said. "We are going in through Main Inlet. What about Fannin?"

"As soon as we saw the PT boat run up on the beach," the Professor answered, "we sent a radio message. The Chief said he would pick up Fannin. He started out there with three police cars. I imagine Fannin is in jail by now—unless something else went wrong."

"Are we going down to the house boat?" Pete asked.

"Yes," Nick answered, "just to see if they need any help. Then the police will drop us all at the boat yard. The Chief promised to have someone call your father and tell him we had found you."

Pete, Nick and the Professor went out on deck as they sped across the harbor toward the factory. Half way across, they heard three shots echo back.

"Listen to that," Pete shouted. "Do you suppose Fannin is fighting it out with the police?"

"Seems hard to believe he would do anything so stupid," Professor Nevins said. "He hasn't a chance."

When the police boat was about three hundred yards from the house boat, the lights of the factory suddenly came on, lighting up the entire area.

"It must be all over," Pete said.

"Sorry you missed the excitement?" Nick asked.

Pete turned. "Not me. I have had enough excitement to last me ten years."

A moment later the boat pulled up to the factory dock and the three of them jumped off. As they ran up the dock, a police car drove away very fast and, when it pulled on to Shore Road, its red light on the roof began to blink.

A moment later, the Chief came around from the back of the factory.

"What happened?" Nick asked him.

"Fannin and Bucko were in the factory, all right. When we told them to come out, Fannin did, but Bucko tried to make a run for the woods." He pointed toward the disappearing police car. "There they go now—one for the hospital and one for the jail."

"Did Fannin admit they were running guns?" Nick asked.

The Chief nodded. "Yes, but we haven't found out yet where he was going to sell them." He turned to Pete. "So you are all right, are you, Pete? I'm glad to hear it."

"I want to tell you how sorry I am," Pete replied. "I was the reason the PT boat almost got away. I was so sure nobody was going to do anything about Fannin that I tried to be a one-man hero."

The Chief nodded. "You are not the first person who has thought the police weren't doing their job. You probably won't be the last!"

Pete remembered something that had bothered him all along. "Chief, why did Fannin act so loud and know-it-all? Seems to me he would not have wanted to draw so much attention to himself."

"The truth is, Pete, that crooks like Fannin are often just plain stupid—even if you would never believe it from watching TV. Oh, they may be clever enough when they plan their crimes, but then they do something dumb and they are caught. Fannin thought we were so out of date here in Hidden Harbor we wouldn't suspect a thing."

"Chief, can the police boat drop us at the boat yard?" the Professor put in. "It is about time Pete checked in with his father. And, Chief, I was just as much to blame as Pete, getting in the way, spying on Fannin as though

Hidden Harbor didn't already have its police to take care of criminals."

When they reached the boat yard a few minutes later, Wesley Dana was sitting on a box on the main dock, with his crutches beside him.

"Well, I guess you had quite a time," his father said as Pete ran up. "Come on to the house. Let's have something to eat and you can tell me all about it."

They started up through the boat yard.

"Boy, am I ever hungry, Dad," Pete said. "Let me just tell you the best part of the story now, and I can finish the rest while we eat."

"What's the best part?" his father asked.

"Out there in that PT boat," Pete said, smiling at his father, "I finally learned how much it can mean to think first, before you act. Believe me, I learned it so well I will never forget it!"

"I would guess," his father smiled, "that maybe you never will."

www.ingramcontent.com/pod-product-compliance
Lightning Source LLC
Chambersburg PA
CBHW020653180626
46816CB00003B/1269